Bucky of Belgravia

Bucky of Belgravia

Alden Douglas

Belgrave Books
Napa, CA

Belgrave Books
2545 Vintage St.
Napa, CA 94558-2547
www.belgravebooks.com

ISBN: 978-0-9909621-0-6

Cover and text design by Bookwrights
Printed in the United States of America

Bucky of Belgravia

ONE

Bucky Newman boarded the red-eye to London wholly confident of success in his first international assignment. Some might have considered this hubris in a young man who had never experienced so much as a college semester abroad, but a run of sweet luck had convinced him that fortune smiled. Eager for the journey to begin, he stowed his laptop and rain-repellent trench coat, then clambered into a center seat near the toilets at the back of the plane. The cramped and vaguely malodorous coop struck him as unworthy of an up-and-coming professional—the firm's tight-fisted travel policies were an insult to top performers. He closed his eyes and renewed his zeal by reciting a comforting mantra: *Senior Manager for Applications Deployment, UK Financial Markets Group.*

Just ten days had passed since the VP in Manhattan called with a rare double windfall: a bump in rank and a coveted overseas post. Sales had won an engagement with an investment house in the City. Certain skills were needed. Someone had to take the wheel. The client, Routhlis Capital, was a traditional British firm in a brave new digital world; to thrive in the storied Square Mile required updating their tired suite of apps, adding high-speed trading, patterns recognition, and predictive tools. It was a tailored fit. No one in New York could touch Bucky with algorithmic scripts, and for once the self-absorbed execs had put in charge a talented go-getter.

When the news got out that he was headed across the pond, a parade of colleagues appeared at his cubicle to offer congratulations and sage advice. Some had actually visited England, and one—a man of uncommon wisdom—had even traveled outside Greater London. They piled their clichés about Britain onto Bucky's cluttered desk: the wretched food and stupendous drinking, the brilliant theater and weeping weather. *They'll slay you with politeness*, one of them warned. *They'll spit in your American face*, said another. *You're in for the time of your life*, he was promised, and then with surprisingly little humor, *If you make it through this you'll be lucky, Bucky.*

He let it all pass without comment, reassured by the perfect logic of his own long march. A decade earlier, when he was seventeen and desperate for a way up and out of Tonawanda, he'd realized that he couldn't sing, dance, play the guitar, or distinguish himself in any game involving a ball. But the Fates had graced him with a special talent—he could program like a demon. Apps flowed like arpeggios from his slender fingers, and his vivid dreams came alive with dancing database schema. On summer internships during his college years, as his mentors grappled with everyday office ware, he mastered the secrets of cloud infrastructure, business analytics, and web and mobile development. He emerged from SUNY–Buffalo with a computer science degree that his parents held up as the Grail, but far more valuable, he had learned to craft securities trading scripts that outfoxed the institutional players. Manhattan followed as the rational next step, five years and fifteen thousand hours of changing code into gold. The firm's appreciation had finally trickled down.

As the big jet powered aloft and began to lurch through the coastal thermals, he felt an urgent need to see his lover's face and form. He squirmed awkwardly in his seat, digging through his pockets until he could get his phone out and begin shuffling through images. He drew the screen tight against his chest, hoping the matron by the window wouldn't catch a telltale glimpse of swelling breasts or alabaster thighs. His snapshots might have revealed an amateur sense of composition, but it didn't matter—Dayna Dauphinais *dans le nu* was all sweeping legs and teasing eyes, her pout suggesting far more interesting pastimes than photography.

He had met her two years after he arrived in Manhattan; she'd managed to parlay a BA in French lit from Vassar into a marketing role at headquarters. Dayna didn't know tech from tacks, but she rhapsodized about Sacré-Cœur and Sainte-Chapelle, the Tuileries and the Petit Trianon and something called *Les Troyens* that was either a pastry or an opera. He was instantly smitten. The first eleven times he suggested drinks after work she sent him scuttling with a head-shaking no. But unyielding persistence wore her down, eventually landing him in her bed. The sex was mechanical at first, then over a torrid summer they discovered all the magic words and forbidden fun. By Labor Day they'd moved into a one-bedroom in Battery Park City.

Bucky threw himself into the affair, his affection quickly morphing into infatuation. Dayna was everything that he was not: well traveled and well dressed, unfazed by men with rank and resources, blithely certain which Spanish *albariño* she wanted with her sea bass. While he struggled to make empty party talk, she bubbled over with hilarious stories—who had hit on whom in the Hamptons, or the one about the crazy captain of the charter yacht, last summer in the Dodecanese. Ordinary girls might 'succeed' in New York, but Dayna flashed and shimmered. He loved it all, and soon he loved her.

Once—in a moment of drunken courage—he had dared to ask what she saw in him. Her eyes narrowed. "It won't do my career any harm to hook up with the brightest guy in the firm."

When his promotion came with a move to London, he was two paychecks away from buying a ring. If Dayna had wrapped her arms around him and whispered, "Please don't leave," he might have torn up his project schedule and penciled in a wedding. But his partner saw a different opportunity for them both.

"Go!" she urged. "This is what you've been working toward all your life. I'll see if they have headcount open in UK campaigns and follow you over. *Il sera parfait.*"

They agreed to split the rent on the one-bedroom while she looked for someone to sublet; with his salary increase and overseas housing stipend, he could pay his share in the meantime and still cover a London flat. Their plan would mean weeks apart—maybe a couple of months—but he assumed that would only make their reunion in London more passionate. He pressed the phone to his heart and imagined himself slipping off to Antwerp for the best price on a ring. When Dayna arrived he would propose dramatically at Tower Bridge or Windsor Castle.

Somewhere over the Irish Sea he scrubbed his face with a steaming little towel, then debarked at London and presented his work permit to Her Majesty's skeptical officers. They glared as if the document heralded only another hungry mouth. In the terminal he bought a train pass from a Sikh with a handheld cellular machine; minutes later he bounded from the Heathrow Express onto the platform at Paddington Station, the laptop swinging from his shoulder and a roll-aboard clattering along behind. Just outside, he assumed, grand castles and regal palaces awaited—Great Britain in full pictorial splendor—but the view from the street was of money changers, souvenir traps, and grimy taverns crowding the far side of Craven Road, the pedestrian swarm appearing equally divided between frantic, rushing tourists and disheveled drunkards with all the time in the world. He tossed his bags into a black cab, covering any qualms by barking the address of his firm's office in the City.

Behind the Plexiglas divider a security camera coolly regarded his wrinkled collar and puffy eyes; a decal below it advised, *Your taxi driver is an Englishman.*

"First time in London, sir?"

The cabbie had made him at a glance, but with a New Yorker's wariness Bucky avoided spilling his story. Instead he muttered something about the station's odd mix of ancient and modern, jumbled together in a way he hadn't expected.

"Well, sir, Paddington became the terminus of the Great Western Railway in 1838, so it's hardly the newest station in London. It was entirely redesigned by I. K. Brunel in 1854. You know Brunel, he's the same man who designed the Clifton Suspension Bridge over the Avon Gorge, and the first propeller-driven transatlantic steamship."

Bucky didn't know Brunel, but he wasn't about to say so. He wondered if the driver might be some scholar laid low by austerity, or one of those drones who earn a living talking the ears off day-trippers. The man looked to be in his forties, unremarkable in a woolen car coat and a Donegal cap; his voice was hoarse from shouting through the oblong hole in the divider.

Bucky thought he'd have some fun, maybe even stump him. "Right, so what did the I. K. stand for?"

"Forgive me, it was Isambard Kingdom Brunel. His father was Sir Marc Isambard Brunel and his mother was Sophia Kingdom. In the early nineteenth century people would pack up the whole family tree with their names. If I'm not mistaken, Brunel was born in 1806 or '08, just before the Regency."

Bucky was almost impressed. "Anything else around here worth seeing?"

"It's endless! Up behind Praed Street is the hospital where Fleming discovered penicillin, and just to the north, on Edgware Road, is a high-security police station where they interrogate captured terrorists. But we won't be going that way.

I'd like to take Bayswater to Marble Arch and then follow Park Lane, if that's all right with you. It will be quicker at this time of the morning."

"Yeah, I'm down with that." Then came the jolt.

"If you don't mind my asking, sir, are you interested in trading algorithms?"

"How the hell could you know—"

"The address you gave me is between the Cheesegrater and the Gherkin, and the firms on your particular block cater to institutional traders. The cutting edge in that line of business is either high-speed transactions or programmed trading of some type. That requires algorithms, and I couldn't help noticing you carry a laptop rather than a tablet. Might you be a developer?"

"Lots of people still carry laptops," Bucky said, as if he were fending off a detective's inquiry. "It doesn't mean I'm on the bench."

"Of course not, sir. I didn't mean to give offense."

As they rounded Westbourne Gate and the expanse of Kensington Gardens opened to the south, he decided not to make an issue of the driver's impertinence. "No offense taken. Are you interested in IT?"

"Among other things. I'm sure that I'm not at your level, but a few years ago I read a book about the early computers built at Bletchley Park to unbutton the German ciphers. It got me going on the subject."

"All vacuum tubes, right?"

"Correct, thermionic valves were all they had available in February of '44, when Colossus One came online. But it was good enough to unravel the key combinations from the Lorenz machines, which allowed the German messages to be read."

"Gotcha."

"And as always, the human side was revealing. A mathematician by the name of Max Newman headed up the

Colossus project. He had a section of more than three hundred specialists—most of them women—which came to be called the Newmanry. Not half bad, wouldn't you say, changing the course of history with one's first invention?"

Bucky didn't answer; the coincidence had jolted him again, particularly since he hadn't mentioned his name to the driver, or heard of this English namesake. His focus shifted outside the cab—the tight corners and high walls of the streets near Paddington had given way to broader, greener views, as they rounded an open curve with a park beyond. He had never wandered outside the borders of America, but he'd seen his share of capitals as film locations. The modern ones had a certain sameness to them that he wasn't finding in the passing streets. There was an indefinable quality to the London landscape and the brick and stone structures that extended along the park. The atmosphere wasn't anything like Manhattan, and he tried to come up with an alternative label, but lacking a vocabulary of architectural styles, he could only conclude that it was all very...*British.*

"That's the Palace coming up on the right, sir. I'm going to head up the Mall and then cut across to the Embankment. Shouldn't be too bad after that. It was a bank holiday yesterday. A lot of people left town." Soon they were motoring through Admiralty Arch and around the lunatic traffic circle, and for the first time Bucky saw the stirring view down Whitehall, the grand clock tower rising in the distance. They jinked onto Northumberland Avenue and surged forward to the Embankment, where across the Thames the Eye turned slowly round. He twisted on the seat to follow its all-but-imperceptible motion, until it disappeared from view as they angled onto Queen Victoria Street. When they stopped at the foot of a gray mid-rise tower, he got out with his bags and pushed a bill through the open window.

"Thank you kindly, sir. My sense is you might need a driver until you're comfortable using the Tube. If you call my mobile number I can pick you up anywhere." He offered a plain white card.

Bucky glanced at it momentarily. The cabbie-savant was Will Beard. The phone number appeared to have too many digits. He thought about asking *What tube?*, thinking it had something to do with their discussion of early computer electronics, but a smartly coifed young woman was waving to him from inside the lobby. He drew himself up and stepped forward at the measured pace he imagined a senior manager might take.

His contact at the London office proved to be a kind of anti-Dayna—a modest model of prim efficiency who insisted on handling the rolling suitcase and shepherding the new manager up to the seventh floor, to his first office-with-a-door. The London bureau was smaller, darker, and more sparsely furnished than the glittering HQ in Manhattan; that was SOP out in what they called "the geographies." IT services was a game of gross margins, and the appalling rents in the City gutted the bottom line. But he found the conference room adequate for his first team meeting. The firm had assigned him a Polish scripting specialist and a tiny Singaporean woman who wrote brilliant Java code, a Jamaican in a Rasta beanie who transformed application interfaces into works of art, and Punjabi and Pakistani systems integrators who had declared a temporary truce. Getting it right with his people was paramount. He had endured years of chilling snobbery from the tiers of management above him—it was the only affront that could still set him off—and he'd told himself that once he had subordinates, he would motivate them with camaraderie and kindness. Sure, every successful manager he'd known had relied upon the proven tools of fear and scornful prickery, but he was certain his cheery way would be better. Already he felt a sense of protective ownership, and remembering the cabbie's anecdotes, he couldn't help but think, *My Newmanry.*

He had worked up a pithy intro to set the right tone. He'd read that in 1942, an American officer told a room packed with British generals, admirals, and air marshals, "We're not going to do much talking until we've done more of the fighting. When we're gone, we hope you'll be glad we came." He planned to offer a clever paraphrase, suggesting that he wouldn't tell his team how to do their jobs until he had proven he could handle his own, then finish with the laugh about their being glad when he'd gone home. But as he confronted a tight ring of confidants, all jabbering incomprehensible Brit-slang, his witty words deserted him. "Let's nail down what the client expects from us," he said tersely, then kicked off a round-the-room and an hour of listening and note-taking. The rep who had won the engagement with Routhlis Capital was on the speakerphone. "Listen, there are two factions at this shop," said his amplified voice. "The younger managers want high-speed trading…the old guard wants to go on playing hide the loot for third-world potentates and petroleum ministers. They'll have to be dragged kicking and screaming."

Operating without sleep, Bucky feared a collapse after lunch. But as the afternoon arrived he burned with inspiration, feeding off the energy of his people. The client's office was only a few blocks away. After a call ahead, he rounded up his two leads and marched down Leadenhall Street to meet them. He expected to walk out onto a trading floor like any in Manhattan, with boulevards of broker workstations and flat-screen monitor galleries, a Babel of English, German, Mandarin, and Arabic swirling up from the traders. Instead Routhlis was a realm of double-locked doors and opaque windows, where market insights were whispered behind screening hands. As they scratched their names into the visitors log, a nervous receptionist asked each of them—individually—if they had signed the strict NDA.

Alistair, the IT director, was six and a half feet tall and so thin that viewed side-on, he all but disappeared. Derek ran the wealth management practice; he was splendidly fat with a hairless head and a soup-stained golden necktie. Bucky felt the tension between them—the sales rep had been right about Routhlis splitting into factions. Whatever clique he cozied up to, the other side would scheme to undermine his work.

"I should like to outline our expectations for this engagement from the perspective of platforms, apps, scripts, and functionalities," Alistair began, glancing nervously at his tablet.

"Bugger that," Derek interrupted. "Functionally, we expect you lot to earn us double whatever you're charging."

Bucky smiled innocently as he sprang the trap. "So if we delivered, say, three hundred percent return on investment, you would agree that we had exceeded your expectations?" He kept a straight face as he waited for an answer, but one of his leads put down his head to hide a smirk.

Only later would the full meaning of the day open up to him. The company was putting him up in a high-rise hotel opposite Kensington Gardens, until he could sort out a flat. From the fifteenth floor, drink in hand, he watched the lights come up along the curving reach of the Thames. To the south he could make out the ivory smokestacks of the old Battersea Power Station, then, flowing seaward, the art deco facade of MI6, the Victoria Tower and the lavender circle of the Eye, the ruby dagger of the Shard and the distant obelisks of Canary Wharf. People loved to talk about the pinnacles in their lives— graduation, marriage, that first miraculous child—but nothing had prepared him for the thrill of seeing London spread before him, certain that here in the grand tableau he had found his place in the world. He recalled the weekend before he started college, walking with his father through the abandoned steel mills south of Buffalo. *Promise me you'll do better than I did*, his old man had pleaded. Now, before him, lay tangible proof that he had kept his promise. Thanks to timing, talent, and luck, he could finally have it all—the job, the girl, the money, the renown, and the brass ring of personal triumph he had reached for ever since leaving Buffalo.

He sat on the edge of the bed and thumbed out a text to Dayna. *Incredible day. Team is solid. Met the client. I've got this covered. London cabbies much smarter than ours. Love ya, B.*

■ ■ ■

At the end of the second week, Routhlis's managing director wanted a progress report over lunch. Bucky had met Morley Cruikshank only briefly during the first days of the project; he was an outsize man in a magnificent suit, with a head of disheveled white hair and a beak-like nose that gave him the look of a fish eagle. Beneath the nose was something less like a mouth than a maw. Cruikshank hadn't let on which faction he favored. He might be waiting it out to see who won, then declare victory either way. He snapped his fingers for Alistair and Derek—the deputies were coming along, probably to speak for the interests of the two camps, Bucky assumed. They walked a short distance to a Northern Italian restaurant where a queue extended out the door. Cruikshank elbowed past the crowd and approached the maître d', instructing him, "*Quattro, per favore, Enzo.*" They were conducted at once to a red leather banquette in a corner.

"So Newman, from all reports you haven't managed to ruin us yet," Cruikshank opened affably. He eyed his two underlings. "I made the right move calling in this lad and his mates, wouldn't you say?"

"Without a doubt, sir."

"Brilliant choice, sir."

"How reassuring that you think so! Anyway, Newman, I fully expected you to shine. Your head man in New York forwarded your CV before he volleyed you over, and I noticed your fine education. The State University of New York at *Buffalo*, I believe? I trust you didn't have to call the cavalry to rescue you from the circling savages."

Bucky pretended to laugh. "When we needed rescue we called the snowplows. Buffalo had a strong technology program, and they offered me financial assistance. So where did you go to school?"

Alistair and Derek blanched at the cheeky question, but Cruikshank answered without hesitation. "Toffeter, then Oxford."

A waiter brought bread and oil, and filled their glasses from a bottle of sparkling water. "*La solita, signore?*" he inquired of Cruikshank, who nodded. He returned with a tumbler filled with clear liquid.

Cruikshank sipped from the glass and a note of juniper berries wafted across the table. "For God's sake have a drink, Newman. This isn't an American corporate cafeteria."

Bucky had always found that lunch was the worst occasion to talk business, especially when the client was drinking, and he had never allowed himself a drop at such times. But he didn't want to appear unsociable, or unfamiliar with British customs. He flagged down the waiter and pointed to Cruickshank's glass. "I'll have the same." It came out quickly, Plymouth Gin with a faint breath of tonic.

"On behalf of our firm, I want to thank you for the opportunity to serve Routhlis Capital. Based on an excellent start, I am completely confident that we will achieve the business goals of this ambitious project. And I have to say, I'm enjoying London so much that I could see myself living here permanently."

Cruikshank plainly recognized the aroma of absolute crap; his eyes hardened as he took the opposite tack from what Bucky had intended. "You might want to reconsider that last part. The Tories may be in power again, but they lost track of their bollocks on the walk over to Whitehall. Taxes are ruinous, it's the NHS and all the other socialist rot. Just because Mrs. Grundy wants her gallbladder out shouldn't mean that I'm personally obliged to pay."

"Damn straight, sir," Derek said around a mouthful of sopping bread.

Now Bucky was glad for the drink. He took a more vigorous pull, searching for a response that was as close to meaningless as courtesy allowed. "People do need health care," was his weak effort.

"They want it is what you mean to say," Cruikshank snapped. "They want all sorts of things. Billions swarm the planet—why, there aren't enough fish in the sea to feed them, much less doctors to treat their scourges. But maybe the pharma doomsayers are right, and some upstart germ will develop an immunity to all our pills. Then we'll get back to a sustainable population."

"From your lips to God's ear," Alistair said brightly, though his pursed lips betrayed apprehension. "If I might have a moment, I wanted to call your attention to the proposed deployment schedule for the high-speed scripts, which will conflict with four trading desk and comms applications upgrades now under way. We should talk about a strategy to mitigate—"

"That's boffin talk. I pay you to deliver monetary results, not drag me down into the bulrushes. And you prevented Newman here from telling us what he thinks of my social philosophy."

Bucky didn't like the way Cruikshank snarled at his people, but at least he wasn't one of them. And he had to admit, a practiced air of superiority wasn't exclusive to the Brits. In

New York, management had bullied one and all into the same servile pose, like the feeding ducks in the corporate pond, heads underwater and tails in the air. He eased a deeper swallow, just to take the edge off. "The consensus in America is that demand rolls up from Main Street. The greater the economic activity at the bottom of the pyramid, the greater the profits at the top."

Cruikshank snorted and took a great swig from his tumbler. "Gladstone said to Disraeli, 'I will back the masses against the classes,' but I'm telling you, Mr. Buckminster C. Newman, in truth the masses are asses."

The waiter returned with salad, serving each of them from a glazed majolica bowl—assorted greens and garbanzos, a few fat tomato wedges, and chopped scallions with a dose of ground pepper. Bucky took the opportunity to put his head down and attack with knife and fork. Something was off, though he couldn't imagine that he had downed enough of the English gin to affect his thinking. Crunching through noisy mouthfuls, he weighed his impressions, seeking professional distance, reminding himself to moderate his tone before responding. "How does that apply to your business activities?" he asked at last.

Cruikshank spoke as if he were explaining to a six-year-old the reason the sky only appeared to be blue. "My father-in-law, Sir Charles Routhlis, gave me some invaluable direction when I joined the firm. It makes no difference whether you're the buyer or seller; it makes *all* the difference whether you're the fucker or fuckee."

Alistair and Derek laughed and drummed their fists on the table. It couldn't have been the first time they had heard this line, but on command they hooted.

Bucky suddenly felt more confident, and he spoke to Cruikshank like a raw younger brother. "That's fine until it's your night in the barrel. Don't you think what goes around is gonna come around?" He washed down his words with more gin.

"No, I expect that the cream shall rise and the sun come up in the east. We have always had an educated class in this country that understood how to build empires, whether of territory or money. We're the reason that Britain is great. We intend to come out on top."

"So the Raj is coming back, and the polo players will run it? Maybe you haven't noticed, but this is the twenty-first century."

Alistair coughed uncomfortably, and Derek lowered his eyes. Cruikshank's hawkish face had broken out in beads of sweat, and he loosened his necktie with a hard tug. "Look, Newman, I'll explain this in a way that even a Yank will understand. Imagine a Victorian woman in a skirt and frilly petticoats. The outermost garment is Sydney, Singapore, and Hong Kong; the layers beneath it are the overseas territories, Grand Cayman, the British Virgins, Bermuda and the rest, all of them tax havens. Closer still, like satin knickers, are the Crown dependencies of Guernsey, Jersey, and the Isle of Man. And at the center, the all-controlling object of desire, our sweet wet flower of London. You may imagine your computer tricks are a path to easy wealth, but they are just a ripple on the sea of cash that flows to us from Britain's Second Empire."

Bucky slammed the last of his gin and banged the glass. "Go tell that to the Brazilians who just passed you up for sixth-place GDP honors. And if you want to know why, it's simple. When you start your day by kissing the royal ass, things tend to go downhill from there."

■ ■ ■

When the VP called from Manhattan, he took the positive approach they had all learned to employ when dealing with disasters. "Good thing you're still early-stage on this project," he began in a tone so upbeat it was almost lilting. "You can hand off to your lead developer and let him fake it until your replacement shows. In the meantime, just jump on the next plane and get the hell out of Dodge."

"*What?*"

"Look, you had a great run with us, five years is a long time with any shop. With your skill set you'll find plenty of short-term gigs until something permanent turns up."

"You're saying I'm fired?"

He answered after a painful silence. "I'm saying if you go quietly, we won't ask payroll for a claw-back against your stock options. But don't come looking for a reference."

Bucky decided to wait until evening before calling Dayna. New York was hours back and he needed the time to compose himself. He began choosing the right affirmations: this was just a bump in the road; they'd be together again sooner than expected; a year from now he'd be back in the driver's seat. But his tired bromides went unexpressed. In minutes Dayna's text flashed on his phone. *Management sez U hurt the firm. Merde, Bucky, qu'est-ce que tu fais?!? And how the f**k will U pay your $hare of the rent?*

He had heard other ruined men—divorced adulterers, Ponzi schemers, candidates caught with their wands in the wind—say their greatest shock wasn't how far they had fallen, but how quickly. Many men had plummeted from vastly greater heights, but he couldn't think of anyone who had gone down faster.

TWO

On a miserable morning two decades earlier, in a cold sodden field near Krasnogorsk, Yuri Pavlovitch Dolgorukov struggled to pour the foundation of a sprawling warehouse park. With his first attempt the slab had failed to cure. In itself this was not enough to discourage him—lesson one at the Moscow Construction Technicum was how to defeat the mud and rain of a Russian autumn. But apart from these familiar adversaries, he had a hidden enemy. A line of trucks dispatched by the usual supplier stood by for the latest pour; when the first opened its sluice gate a flood of gray slop cascaded down and splattered into a space defined by wooden forms. The concrete spread rapidly, nudged along by Yuri's crew with their pole trowels. Truck after truck vomited out its load, and one of the laborers flashed a hand signal as the mix reached half the required depth. At that moment a shining ZIL driven by a liveried chauffeur arrived at the project trailer. Yuri signaled a halt to the pour, and began to jog—then run—toward the limousine; when the rear door opened he skidded to a stop and came to rigid attention. He had never met the oligarch on whose project they toiled, but no one could fail to recognize the great man as he emerged. The Boss wore a sable hat and a double-breasted topcoat, and he was smoking a slim brown cigarette with an odor like oily horseshit. His burnished shoes gleamed atop the muck. He flicked away some annoying ash, then cleared his throat and nodded toward the line of cement trucks.

"Can't you see the pig is watering down every load?"

Reeling, Yuri made for the trailer and seized a cone and rod for a slump test. He had been on the job less than a year. His beloved beauty, the round-faced Zhanna, was pregnant with their first child. If he were to be fired for lack of care, both would freeze and starve. When the slump collapsed before him, confirming the bloated water content of the cement, he cursed the supplier under his breath, then more bitterly cursed himself for a naïve fool.

The oligarch, N. V. Klepakov, spoke to him in a steely voice. "There are only two kinds of men in this world—*lokhi* and *suki*. You must decide which one you will be, Yuri Pavlovitch." The two choices were "fuckers" and "their bitches."

"Da, Nicolai Vasilievitch!"

Klepakov cast his foul cigarette into the mud, then pushed his hand down the front of his pants and gave his private organs a shake, adjusting the hang to his liking. The hand came out again and he vanished into the ZIL.

That night, in an alley behind a bar in Kuntsevo, Yuri posed a simple question to the cement supplier: *How will you drive a truck with no testicles?* In the aftermath only proper material was delivered. And pleased by this outcome, the oligarch gave Yuri a role in each of his future projects. Through the nineties and the first decade of the new century they built highways and apartment blocks, stadiums and office space, industrial parks and sprawling, sybaritic dachas for the men who controlled the new Russia. The commercial structures were inanimate cubes of steel and glass and wire, but in the magnificent dachas Yuri discovered his second love. Building out the sumptuous interior spaces, he learned to weave magic with exotic hardwoods and hand-laid Italian tile; the full powers of marble, limestone, and travertine came under his inspired control. When Klepakov looked to the West and built his first palace in Mayfair, he brought Yuri to London as construction manager, instructing him to harness his talents and put to shame all rivals. Three more mansions followed in Knightsbridge, Hampstead, and on a hilltop in Richmond overlooking the Thames. Now a new project—different from the others—had been entrusted to Yuri's capable hands. It was a further rung up on a long ladder, and one that might even allow him to bring Zhanna and their sons to Britain.

Yuri closed his mouth around a blini topped with caviar, then washed it down with icy vodka. The Tottenham pub near the rail line was his favorite English watering hole, a shadowy place with unvarnished tables and grimy floors where working men drank to oblivion. When a young American with copper hair and a freckled face stumbled in from the street, Yuri paid little attention; the kid collapsed onto a barstool and wedged his black computer case behind the boot rail, then motioned to the indifferent bartender. Yuri watched him bang glass after glass of dark ale for nearly an hour, knocking it back as if it were Coca-Cola. Desperation had a smell he could detect at a hundred paces, and its odor filled the pub.

He waited a while, biding his time, feeling his certainty grow, then approached the boy, appearing suddenly by his side. "I have watched you drink, *tovarish*. Either you are great lover of Newcastle Brown, or you are running away from something."

Bucky looked up without answering. The Russian had a bullet head and bony ridges above his eyes. The stain of a neck tattoo crept from under his collar. His hair was still wavy and thick but his broken teeth were heavily discolored, and he had reached the point in life at which a thin layer of flab had spread like sugar icing over the underlying musculature. Though he moved like a man in his thirties, the furrows to either side of his mouth belonged to someone older.

Again the Russian tried to break the ice. "Many men run from police, from women, from cruelties of life. Is it not better to forget our troubles and share vodka and caviar? It is Huso Malossol, I promise there is none better." He spooned the glistening black roe onto an unsalted cracker, then filled a shot glass with Moskovskaya. "You try, then swallow with this."

Bucky ate and drank. The caviar was superb but the cheap vodka burned his veins and spun his head in loopy circles.

"I am Dolgorukov," the Russian declared, thumping his solid chest. "Call me Yuri Pavlovitch." He knocked an unfiltered Sobranie cigarette halfway out of a pack and held it up. "You wish? Owner does not enforce smoking ban." When it was refused, he pulled the cigarette out with his teeth and lit it with a Zippo.

"Bucky Newman."

"Why you come to London? Salivate on crown jewels? Make pilgrimage to Madame Tussauds?"

"I was here on business. I haven't had time for any sightseeing trips to goddamn Buckingham Palace."

The Russian seemed to take no notice of the harsh tone; he sipped his vodka in an unhurried way and then continued. "You miss little. Parliament is commendable structure, Palace only so-so. As for the rest, all is gray, beige, brown, white. Czars had richer sense of color—exterior walls of azure, yellow, turquoise, and ocher, layering gilt as if gold were tin. You know palace of Ekaterina Velikaya, in St. Petersburg?" Bucky shook his head uncertainly. "In Hermitage is Malachite Room, with columns of magnificent green. Golden doors, draperies like blood, Italian ceiling, mosaic floor. This is how immortals build, and it is only one room of a thousand! But I tell you, in my country there is splendor all about. Fountain terraces of the Summer Palace. Golden domes of the Novodevichy, in Moscow. I am no believer, but those domes make me want to pray."

Bucky regarded him suspiciously, taken aback by the effusive lecture. A conversation with some prolix Russian expat was the last thing he wanted. Through the ale and now the vodka, the day was still a painful blur. After the firing he had shot from the office in a rage, stamping the length of Cannon Street with his laptop wildly swaying; he damned the City and the Second Empire, Morley Cruikshank and his gas-passing in-laws, and every posturing prick on both sides of the Atlantic. Farther down, the monumental bulk of St. Paul's had loomed above him, and he felt an awful impulse to bolt into the cathedral and beg for sanctuary. But as he recalled that it wasn't a Catholic church, the soaring cupola and towers were transformed into battlements, and he imagined that from their heights, enemies might fire down upon him. The colossal stones seemed to come to life, shouting out, *You're nothing!* What followed was a blind escape through ancient alleys and confusing lanes, as he fled from the intimidating grandeur of central London. Beneath a leaden sky he tramped through Clerkenwell and Shoreditch, Canonbury and Stoke Newington. Here, to the north of moneyed London, the striped suits and lizard shoes abruptly vanished, replaced by stained denim and torn leather, *dishdasha and kufi*. Ordinarily he might have worried for his laptop—even for his safety—but he ghosted down these alien streets, unseen and unacknowledged. Still he trudged on, through Stamford Hill and then into Tottenham. At nightfall his thirst had driven him into the pub.

Now the Russian was blathering again, wheedling for a further opening, "If it is business that brings you here, perhaps we may have interests in common. London is land of opportunity, as you Americans like to say."

"Maybe for some," Bucky muttered without interest.

Dolgorukov tried another angle. "To be sure…not every man would be king. But are we not driven by love, as well as ambition?"

"How's that?"

"My faithful wife and three fine sons remain in Krasnogorsk. When plans succeed, we shall reunite in London. And for you, *tovarish*, surely there must be a girl?"

Bucky told him about Dayna, how they had met at the firm, moved in together, how he hoped to marry her. As Dolgorukov plied him with more caviar and vodka, the whole story of his rise from Buffalo to Manhattan to London tumbled out, almost as a confession—the pledge he had made to his failed father; the talent that had blossomed at college; the successes he'd tallied on a hundred projects for securities firms on the Street. Then, after intending to omit the catastrophe at Routhlis Capital, the arc of the story forced him to reveal how he had been undone by gin and his own loose tongue.

Curiously, Dolgorukov interrupted at every point with questions, or to ask for more details, almost as if he were conducting an employment interview. Bucky assumed he didn't know any better than to pry, or perhaps his interrogating style was intended to prove that the sad, strange tale wasn't boring him. Dolgorukov raised his glass, then wiped his mouth with his sleeve. "You are not the first man to feel the boot of his master. But take heart, there is hope for your plans, and even for your beloved! Imagine that men might build in London with all the splendor of Russian royalty, commanding style and substance without petty limitations. Can you envision a legacy lasting for centuries, at the heart of Europe's greatest city?"

"Sure I can…if somebody coughs up millions to pay for it."

Dolgorukov leaned closer as if he meant to share a confidence. "I have good fortune to serve true giant, a great oligarch who outshines any Czar. I am London construction manager for his many projects. We complete superb *pied-à-terre* only last month. I promise you, Romanovs never lived so well as my patron Nicolai Vasilievitch Klepakov."

Bucky's ears went up with suspicion. "Where does his money come from?"

"Petroleum, timber, nickel, diamonds…other commodities of reliable value." The Russian fished in an inner pocket of his coat and brought out a handful of rectangular metallic tiles, scattering them casually onto the bar. In the smoky light of the pub they appeared to be pieces from a game, like dominoes. "You know this metal, palladium? Nicolai Vasilievitch owns many lucrative mines. Sometimes I am paid in this way. It is safer than paper money, and the Crown levies no thieving taxes."

Bucky lifted one of the palladium tiles into a better light. The metal was near to silver in color, but without the hard mirror shine; instead it glowed with the rich subtlety of gold. The bar had real heft, and he turned it over to examine the hallmark:

палладий

999.5

10 унция

"Numbers mean palladium is nearly pure, and weight is ten ounces. How do you say, 'Is more where that comes from.' I favor this expression!"

"So now what? Another private palace?"

"No, *tovarish*. For my service, I am rewarded with rare opportunity. Nicolai Vasilievitch counts among his properties an archaic home on Belgrave Square, which he seeks to employ to greater advantage. He bids me to transform this house into private gentlemen's club, where the elite may enjoy fine gaming and drinking in an atmosphere of elegance. My patron shall keep one quarter of proceeds for himself, and savor the many pleasures of the house. All other monies flow to me. Is this not the generosity of a noble captain?"

"London is thick with gentlemen's clubs. Most are dives,

and the good ones are for titled toffs whose grandfathers went to Eton. Who's gonna pay to join your club?"

Dolgorukov shrugged, as if this were no obstacle. "Members will be the super-rich, the glamorous and famous. We shall cater to titans who manipulate the levers of state power, to finance ministers, telecom bosses, Malaysian playboys and Kazakh pop stars. Nigerian oilmen and Chinese real estate barons will sing our praises around the globe. Naturally we will welcome many Brits of the uppermost class. MPs and senior military officers, High Court judges and peers with influence at Whitehall will find themselves at home in our society."

"What makes you think your club could pull a crowd like that? Those people can drink and gamble wherever they want."

"Is true, I admit. But we shall have competitive advantage. In our magnificent mansion, men of success and tasteful women will enjoy sincere exchange and joint satisfaction of interests."

Bucky stared blankly, trying to decode the stilted phraseology through his drunken haze. Then in a rush he understood. "You're freakin' nuts! You think you can open a high-end brothel in central London and disguise it as a private club? You'll never get away with it."

"Every city has houses of pleasure. As to how they come to exist, men speak in earnest, understandings are reached, monies paid, permissions given."

"Try that out with Scotland Yard."

Dolgorukov's gaze sharpened. "Police are men like you and me, they desire wealth and pleasure. Remember what is true of matter and energy—these things are interchangeable! I promise you, money and sex are interchangeable with many useful things. Men who offer both to the world can ask for anything in return, even from police."

"Have you even thought this through? You'd need to set up a legal entity as a cover. What about building permits and inspections? Do you realize how hard it's going to be to get a liquor license for a residential property?"

Dolgorukov held up a hand to stop him. "Money and sex, sex and money, all barriers will fall before their powers. In truth, there is but one conundrum that delays full accomplishment of plan. As you can see, I speak the perfect English, but writing not so good. I must have partner to review printed bills and contracts—a man who is knowing computers and how to bring service to market. My patron Nicolai Vasilievitch wishes to remain at a distance from certain delicate matters, as do I. Far better for the partner that I speak of to hire alluring girls for house, and accomplish various technical duties." He pointed to Bucky's nylon laptop case, wedged against the bar. "You can make website and mobile app, yes?"

"In my sleep."

"As expected," Dolgorukov said with a dismissive wave. "I leave these matters to you. Construction and gaming, you leave to me." He inclined his head toward the back of the pub, indicating that he was stepping away for a piss.

Bucky saw his chance to escape, and he rocked unsteadily to his feet. His head was spinning, but deep within his brain was a compact kernel of rationality that still seemed to function. It wouldn't have allowed him to write error-free code or keep a car in a lane, yet somehow he felt the decision before him was one he could weigh with confidence. He had encountered all sorts in New York, but he had never before called a Russian his friend; the Arcadys and Anatolis who had taken over Brighton Beach had a bad reputation for trauma. Setting that aside still left the bigger political picture: long after the Cold War, dark enmity still lingered. How could the Russkies ever be trusted? Didn't they have thousands of missiles aimed at Manhattan and other valuable precincts? Dolgorukov seemed a decent guy, but he was at one with the smoke and soot of the pub. This was his comfort zone, despite the hot air about an oligarch's palaces. He talked a good game, but would likely fold if his bluff were called.

When he returned, Bucky spoke with the downtown edge he employed when people needed pushing. "So you're serious about this? You're asking me to come in with you as an equal partner? I wouldn't consider anything less than a fifty-fifty revenue split."

To his amazement, the Russian didn't back away. "Da, fifty-fifty, that is it exactly."

With all the coldness he could summon, Bucky threw out the ultimate deal-breaker. "Yeah, right…but I don't suppose you have any development capital?"

"You doubt that I am man of word? I will show you Dolgorukov is no liar!" He seized Bucky's hand and turned it palm up, then slapped down three of the palladium bars. "Exchange for cash tomorrow, then call and we will meet at house."

He scribbled his mobile number and the Belgrave Square address onto a paper napkin, as Bucky—shocked nearly to sobriety—dropped the palladium bars into his pocket. In the street Dolgorukov exclaimed, "You will make excellent Yankee partner," then wrapped Bucky in a powerful hug and kissed him on the mouth.

"Sodding queers, we'll kick your arse!" a voice threatened from the shadows, and hearing the swift approach of hobnailed boots, Bucky and Yuri ran like hedgehogs.

THREE

Bucky awoke the next morning to his new life as a pimp. Staring bleary-eyed at the ceiling, he felt only baffled amusement. Ordinarily the idea of becoming a cathouse boss instead of an IT consultant would have been madcap stuff, but with all that had happened the previous day it now seemed comically astute. Then he heard the chiding voice of guilt. Over the years he had tried to throw off the burden of his parochial education, telling himself that the *real* apostles were Copernicus, Kepler, Lavoisier, and Heisenberg. He even enjoyed playing a mental game of debunking Augustine and Aquinas. Still the catechism showed up uninvited in his darker moments of doubt. With a wince he recalled how Brother Terrence at Our Lady of Niagara had warned him about the deadly nexus of avarice and lechery. Therein, he vowed, a careless soul would quickly find damnation. The modern world's busiest intersection of greed and lust wasn't hard to locate; the fattest slice of Internet traffic was porn and hookup dating, and the people who filmed or coded it had grown obscenely rich. The thought of entering that arena had never tempted him—*What would I tell my parents?*—but he privately admired the slick page layouts of the .xxx sites, and the ease with which a foot fetishist or someone into pony play could search for nearby partners, between the ages of nineteen and twenty-nine, with blonde hair and green eyes, all for an auto-billed monthly fee. Whatever you thought about it morally, it was killer web development.

But this wasn't going to be cybersex, spun up by anonymous webmasters. His streetwise Russian partner meant to offer flesh-and-blood girls to paying punters. That was bracing stuff. Yet as he measured the sins of the flesh against the cunning travesties he had witnessed in his Wall Street years, entering the high-end British sex trade appeared by far the lesser evil. In Manhattan every investment house kept a trick bag stuffed with scams: equities pump-and-dumps, IPO giveaways for friendly officeholders, trillions in bundled mortgage paper that they sliced and diced and eased up the backsides of gullible governments and pension funds. And the markets could be savage. Years earlier, while optimizing a client's trading website, he had overheard muffled whispers about someone called "the Westport widow." That evening over mojitos a broker spilled the details. A ninetysomething widow owned a block of shares in one of the oil giants, left by a husband who had reached the upper strata of the firm. The stock was all that remained of her man; she refused to sell the bulk of her shares and diversify. To lessen the risk, the brokerage insisted on entering a stop-loss order, reasoning that it would sweep her out of the position in case of a market meltdown. One calm afternoon a malfunction of exchange computers spiraled into a flash crash, and for a moment, share prices for hundreds of issues fell to one cent. The stop-loss order triggered, and the widow's shares vanished in a twinkle of electrons, at a penny apiece.

Everyone assumed the exchange would unwind the trade—but the transaction stood. The brokerage dispatched a fixer and a litigator from Manhattan out to Fairfield County, to break the monstrous news. The widow died a day later.

Bucky kicked off the duvet and swung his feet off the bed. If this was the brutal way of the world, who could call him out for seizing a lucrative opportunity? He was sick of shining boots for his betters, and Yuri's scheme made perfect sense from a risk-management perspective. He wouldn't be contributing any capital of his own, and if the worst happened—a criminal arrest—he would likely pay a fine and be deported back to New York, with the Brits buying the ticket. No one in Manhattan would ever find out, much less care.

He recalled Dayna's text from the previous day. After her bitter response to his firing, he had dashed off a string of messages expressing hope, affection, determination. He retrieved his phone from the nightstand, hoping for an encouraging reply. Her answer was silence. Rising, he next remembered Yuri's gift, folded into his hand before they left the pub, and he tore through his jacket until he found the three palladium bars. They were no drunken delusion. He knew roughly where the spot prices of gold and silver stood, but palladium was a mystery. A trading app on his phone summoned a quote; the ten-ounce bars were worth thousands of dollars each, or in total, he reckoned, a solid two months' contracting time. Another search and he had the address of a retail bullion exchange, not far from what had briefly been his office. He showered, dressed in a rush with his hair still wet, and went out the door.

"I have five competitors in the City," said the Israeli at the metals exchange, when Bucky tried to haggle. "I know their rates, and they know mine. If you have an hour to waste, you might save 50p. Or I can give you 14,839 effing quid right now. You choose."

Bucky said he'd take the cash and handed over the palladium bars. When the clerk returned, he realized the stack of bills was too thick for his wallet. He folded the cash into a choking wad and with difficulty shoved it into his largest pocket.

He texted Yuri, *See you at the house.* Seconds later came a response, *Da.* Then he stepped into the street and phoned the taxi driver he had met on his first day in London.

"There's a coffee bar in the next block to the south of you," Will Beard said, as if he could see it. "Perhaps you'd like to wait there until I arrive?"

In the cafe, wolfing a croissant and a strong bitter latte, Bucky thought about college. At twenty, immersed in the purity of logic and code, he had imagined a life that would allow him to tell the absolute truth, do absolute good, and be regarded as absolutely beyond reproach. That was the miracle of universities, the ability to live in the abstract. Here in the real world, a man had two choices: fucker or fuckee, a one or a zero. Maybe the bastard Cruikshank had done him a favor by revealing the binary clarity of it all. Maybe what he needed was a rough shove into the mountain stream of life, where he would come fully awake and get busy grabbing up his share. He was back on top of his game now—the ale-and-vodka hangover that had clouded his awakening had abruptly disappeared. And filled with sudden resolve, he reaffirmed the choice he had made at the pub, convinced that in a world of broken widows and bend-over frauds, the sins he now intended to commit were venial, and therefore forgivable even by Brother Terrence.

Beard arrived as the last of the latte went down. Bucky told him he was meeting a colleague at the Belgrave Square address, and that he wanted the cab to wait.

"That won't be a problem, sir. I must say, I envy you getting a look at the inside of any residence in Belgravia. It's likely to be posh. May I ask the occasion?"

"We're scouting a location for a private gentlemen's club. Strictly elite clientele. My associate is an expert in construction and gaming." The LED on the cabbie's mounted camera reminded him that his white lies were being recorded. He assumed the system was a deterrent to stickups, and that Beard wouldn't mind turning it off for a known fare. "Can I talk you into shutting off that videocam? Trust me, I don't need to hold you up for cash today."

Beard laughed merrily. "Actually it's not running, apart from that red light you see to the left of the lens. The value of recording a robbery would be limited. The police might find the bugger, but you can be certain he would have spent every penny by that time. The whole point is to have the other man *believe* he's being filmed, and allow his mind to suggest the grim possibilities. Perhaps you've noticed the CCTV cameras around London?"

"They're hard to miss."

"Indeed, but they rarely catch anyone, their purpose is intimidation. If you think about it, whatever miracles we ascribe to technology, human nature wields the greater power."

They had come out of the tunnel on Upper Thames Street and were motoring westward on the Embankment. Bucky decided to raise another subject, still galling him after the previous day's lunch table blowup with Cruikshank. "So why the obsession with class in Britain? It can't be a matter of law?"

Now Beard put on his scholar's cap. "Actually, any wig in the House of Lords would tell you different, never mind the royals. But let me offer you a frame of reference. You've seen the Globe Theatre, on the Southwark side by the Tate? It's a reconstruction of course, but the Globe always had a seating hierarchy. First and best the Lords' Rooms, behind and above the actors, and looking down upon them. Next the Gentlemen's Rooms, which were balconies to the left and right of the stage. The Galleries filled out the rest of the Theatre…cheaper seats, but you didn't get a cushion. Finally there were the pits—in Shakespeare's time just a dirt floor surrounding the stage— filled with groundlings packed together cheek-by-jowl. The old Globe had no toilets, so when nature called, the lords and gentlemen and shopkeepers in the Galleries took their relief at the river's edge. But the groundlings were trapped where they stood, pissing into each other's boots. That's why in the heat of summer they were called the stinkards."

They rounded the curve by Waterloo Bridge and bounced past the Ministry of Defence. Beard finally made his point as Parliament came into view. "Some claim that Britain is more egalitarian today, that the lords and the middle class cheer the same football clubs and ride the same trains through the Chunnel to France. But I can tell you that one thing hasn't changed. There's precious little joy for the stinkards."

West of Parliament they crawled past Victoria Station and continued to Belgrave Square, where Beard began to slowly circle the Inner Ring Road. On all sides were stately blocks of cream-and-tan buildings of several floors, their facades richly ornamented with Romanesque arches or columns topped by elaborate stone capitals. Across the Ring Road in a verdant park stood bronze statues of Leonardo, Columbus, Bolivar, and Prince Henry the Navigator. Flags of many nations flew above the entry porticos, and Beard began ticking off the embassies: Norway, Serbia, Bahrain, six or eight more along the other sides. Despite the serene elegance of the square—or maybe because of it—Bucky sensed that something was wrong. He thought it might be smarter not to locate in an area that would be closely watched by police and private security. Then the genius of it hit him. Belgrave Square was the last place on the planet that anyone would expect to find a house of ill repute.

He leaned toward the hole in the Plexiglas. "Go around again. I want to take it all in." Once more they circled the square; at one corner, the German Embassy occupied a row of formerly separate structures. A black-red-gold flag fluttered in a light breeze above the entry. Beside that compound was an unidentified dwelling that resembled a New York brownstone, but of a lighter color. Yuri Dolgorukov appeared on the steps, arms crossed, his eyes obscured by sunglasses. He was recognizable at once as the man Bucky had met the night before, but in the unforgiving light of day he looked older and rougher.

"This is your address, sir. I'll wait an hour and if you're not out, I'll phone."

As Bucky exited the cab, Yuri opened the heavy black door of the residence, using one of scores of keys on a metal ring. He held out an usher's hand. "After you, *tovarish*."

Entering, Bucky sensed at once that the mansion was deserted. A chill confirmed that the heat had been off for days, and an eerie silence hung about the place; as they moved from the cavernous entry hall into an adjacent salon, his fingers left ski lines in the dust on a credenza. His expectations had been raised, but wandering from room to room and then up a creaking staircase to the first floor, the second, and higher, he felt only disappointment. This time Beard had been wrong. The property wasn't posh so much as past its useful life. It was hardly falling down—the structure appeared to have been built to stand for ages—but the cramped chambers, outdated baths, and faded eighties furniture gave it the air of a museum exhibit, depicting how people had lived in an age before the world got wired.

He groused to Yuri, "This is dismal. I was expecting something flashier."

"Perhaps, but on this canvas we shall paint masterpiece. Have no worries, all that you see will be replaced with grandeur."

Bucky's expression fell. "You're gonna gut the place? How long will that take?"

"Not so long as with British laborers. I have men of every skill and talent who know nothing of trade union rules. If required, one shift works through the day, and another through the night. As for 'weekends' or ridiculous bank holidays, these are absurdities to such men."

"What's your plan, something more modern?"

Yuri held up his open hands in a gesture of futility. "Would you recognize difference between Georgian and Palladian? Baroque and Rococo? Do you understand concept of architectural form as metaphor?"

"Hell no."

"Then perhaps it is best for design to be appreciated upon completion. Have faith…this is not my first mansion."

At the mention of trust, Bucky remembered the thousands of pounds singing in his pocket; it seemed only right to acknowledge the advance. "I exchanged those bullion bars for cash. Look, I appreciate your generosity, but how did you know I wouldn't just take the money and run?"

Now Yuri's eyes sparkled like an old card sharp's. "You are expert of computers, yes? I am expert of knowing who will lie, who will cheat, who will try to screw your dogs and daughters. It was not hard to determine your nature, *tovarish*. A man who fears even British police cannot possibly be a thief."

Stung by the backhanded compliment, Bucky turned away. Then he remembered how his fortunes had changed overnight. Thanks to Yuri he was now a principal. He had always dreamed of running his own shop, of calling himself an entrepreneur, but he had assumed that such an opportunity lay far off in the future. Here was his chance to be a stakeholder, and to bank the lion's share that ownership rightly claimed. He wasn't certain how he would spin it to Dayna or his family, but the gist would be plain: he had hit the jackpot. He smiled without exposing any teeth and grasped Yuri's hand before his new partner could embrace him.

As he returned to Beard's waiting cab, it occurred to him to check the property history. He found an online database of

London public records; the address they had just inspected was owned outright by some outfit called the Dzerzhinsky Group. The last date of sale was barely a month earlier, and the lack of any lien against the property meant that the deal had been all cash.

"And was the residence to your satisfaction?" Beard inquired as they snaked through Knightsbridge, heading back to Bucky's hotel.

"My colleague says we'll have to remodel top to bottom. It needs a ton of work."

"That could be daunting, I suppose. But perhaps it suggests an idea…"

■ ■ ■

That evening, from his hotel room, Bucky dispatched a smug status update to Dayna. She had ignored his earlier messages, but he was certain this latest note would have her rushing to apologize. *Didn't take long to land the next gig. Got recruited by a private equity firm to head up IT & operations on a major London project. Comp is stellar, I hit 'em up for two months in advance. No rest for the wik-kid, and no worries about our rent.*

He knew the money mattered to Dayna—as in big-time. Ms. Dauphinais had no intention of slumming it through life. He hadn't realized the appetites he was up against until they'd spent a weekend with her parents in Poughkeepsie. He'd heard about swells with lawn sculptures and lap pools, but had never before come face-to-face with Sèvres porcelain and Tabriz carpets, programmed lighting and servants in matching uniforms. In a glass-walled breakfast room, as a cook offered poached eggs and mimosas, Dayna's mother inquired if he was one of the Greenwich Newmans.

When he confessed the truth about Tonawanda, Daddy

Dauphinais looked up from the *Journal*, asking nonchalantly, "Is your family in steel?"

Bucky decided at once that this *ensemble élevée* could lift him up into a brighter world—a place where people not only viewed the latest films, but knew the actors by their first names, and dined with the directors. With their advice and support, he could become the kind of man whose conversation moved effortlessly from Chopin to Degas to Gustave Eiffel; the sort of culturally credible sophisticate who wouldn't be laughed at if he turned up in a tux at a Lincoln Center gala.

But on the Sunday train back to Penn Station, Dayna delivered a sobering verdict. "My parents think *tu péter plus haut que son cul.*" He stared dumbly until she added a loose translation: "You're out of your league, Bucky boy."

Now, his head denting the pillow as he drifted toward sleep, he let his thoughts range over all that had happened since he left New York. Somewhere on the edge of dreams his subconscious began to weave the cloth of meaning. Suddenly he was high above London, flying down the curves of the Thames, joined by a flock of ravens that had made their escape from the Tower. He marveled as Will Beard climbed up and out of Shakespeare's Globe on a ladder that reached to the clouds, while from the City side, Morley Cruickshank's mocking voice boomed out, "Bucky, unlucky, Bucky, fuckee!" Then London vanished and he was somehow back in Battery Park, naked with Dayna in their tiny bedroom. He reached for her, wanting love, needing urgently to reconfirm their plans...

But she scowled and pulled away, huffing, "I won't settle for a stinkard."

FOUR

Will Beard's unexpected call came too early the next morning. With his phone set to vibrate a dozen times before rolling to voice mail, Bucky answered only at the eleventh rattle. The cabbie wanted to drive him out to Berkshire, where he had entrée to the estate of some duchess; he claimed there was much to learn from the refinement of the duchess's digs that might come in handy on the Belgrave Square renovation. The clincher was that the ride would be off the meter, and "Her Grace" had promised a light lunch. There had been no further word from Yuri, and in the meantime, he could do as he pleased. He told Beard to collect him at the front of the hotel.

All the way out from London, Beard expanded on his learned commentaries. Their progress along Cromwell Road gave rise to a dissertation on Roundhead rule and the New Model Army, extending through the meandering curves of the Thames, west of Battersea Park. Passing Richmond, Beard declared that Kew, lying just to the south, boasted a botanical garden with the world's largest collection of plants. And a puzzle made it more intriguing. "There are more than thirty thousand living plants on the grounds and in the greenhouses—in total, some six hundred and twenty families of plants—you have your angiosperms, conifers, cycads, all the ferns, the mosses and liverworts, but not one blessed daisy has a Latin family or species name beginning with the letter Y. Now if you consider the English names, there's the yew, yellowhorn, Yunnan banana, and so forth, but you'll search in vain for a Y at the start of any Latin name, at Kew. That fact has confounded me for several years, though I hope to uncover the reason behind it."

Bucky wasn't getting it. "Good luck! I have no idea how you remember it all."

"The trick with memory is to find the points where the strands connect, that's how you'll come to see the hidden patterns. A book or a garden or an episode from history may be mildly interesting on its own, but it's only going to change your life if you take in the interconnected scheme. As Othello says to Desdemona, 'There's magic in the web of it.'"

"I never read *Othello*. But there's got to be more to it than some spiderweb. What's your real secret?"

"My brain changed," Beard said after a pause. "Though I didn't realize the nature of the changes until a neurologist at the Royal Hospital Chelsea explained the details."

"Jeez, I'm sorry. Was it a tumor?"

"Nothing so dire! You see, three or four years of dogged study are required to master the Knowledge and pass the exam for your Green Badge, before you can begin driving a cab in central London. The area you must come to know covers more than one hundred square miles, and within it are twenty-five thousand streets and almost as many places of interest, whose names and locations must be memorized. During my third year of study I began having nasty headaches, and the doctor explained to me that tests had been undertaken on other drivers with the same complaint. The mental labor of acquiring the Knowledge had caused their brains to grow, like a bodybuilder lifting weights. My headaches were caused by that growth."

Bucky was back on more familiar territory. "I thought we were born with all the neurons we'll ever have."

"That was the common belief for decades, but now they're not so sure. The doctors told me the number of neurons in the brains of male canaries increases during the mating season, when they learn new songs to attract females. And they found that among London taxi drivers, the hippocampus becomes enlarged as we acquire the Knowledge. But in my case, the effect was more than just a powerful memory. I began to sort out all manner of mysteries that had stumped me since I was a boy."

"Like what?"

"Well, I'm mechanical by nature, so any sort of engineering has always come easily, but Shakespeare might as well have been written in Greek. Then one evening after I had passed the exam and started driving, a couple straight from the theater started going on in the back of the cab, first the bird saying, 'Who woo'd in haste and means to wed at leisure, I told you, I, he was a frantic fool.' Then the bloke answers back, 'Upon my life, Petruchio means but well, whatever fortune stays him from his word.' Then her again, 'Would Katharina had never seen him, though!' And to my amazement, it was as clear to me as a headline in the *Daily Mirror*."

"What does all that mean?"

"It boils down to him being a jackass for not marrying her in good time. But I still had no idea of the source, so I recited the lines to a bookseller in my borough. He said to me, 'That's Act III, Scene II of *The Taming of the Shrew*.' He sold me a used paperback copy for 70p, and I took it home and read the play. By God, sir, I understood every line, and not just the words but the feelings behind them! I went back and got *Richard III, Romeo and Juliet,* and *A Midsummer Night's Dream,* and read them with the same pleasure, and on and on 'til soon enough I had read them all."

"You read all of Shakespeare?"

"Correct, all the plays, and later the sonnets and the poetry. But it was the plays that enabled me to start hosting my Shakespeare parties."

"At your home?"

"No, here in the cab! It's a game I play inside my head. I imagine a room filled with Shakespeare's characters, and what they would say and do over the course of an evening. Now there are twelve hundred and twenty-four characters in the plays, so there's no end to the combinations. I started with the obvious ones, like all the rulers—just imagine Caesar and Antony pulling Lear into a corner to warn him about what's coming. Then I started mixing up the guest lists, and letting them chat each other up. Think what wisdom Cleopatra might whisper to Miranda in the ladies' toilet, or picture Shylock conspiring with Lady Macbeth to take over all the tabloids in Britain. It's endless fun as you're driving around."

Bucky had never met anyone who had read all of Shakespeare, and the idea of someone manipulating twelve hundred characters and their voices in his head was inconceivable.

But Beard wasn't finished. "Naturally I enjoy reading many other things, now that my brain has improved enough to take them in. London is awash in libraries and books. On my free time I like to pick out two or three interesting volumes and page through them."

"How long have you been doing this?"

"I've been driving for twenty-four years, so I suppose roughly twenty-odd. I've read physics from Newton to Hawking, economics from Adam Smith to John Maynard Keynes, and art history from the Mesopotamians to Miró. In my thirties I discovered what fun world history can be, and thus far I have progressed through the mid–twentieth century. There is always more to learn."

"Have you ever considered becoming a university professor?"

Beard sighed, "I'm afraid it would never work out. I lack the killer instinct."

■ ■ ■

The Duchess of Saltaire's estate at Westerley Park was a portal to a far planet, where the laws of time and money seemed not to apply. On an expanse of flowered fields, watered by lakes swimming with white and black swans, stood a Georgian manor of tremendous breadth and scale. At the northern side of the property were a carriage house and stables; in the gardens that bordered the lakefront, tall topiaries mimicked poodles, pagodas, and giraffes. Bucky had seen postcard photos of palaces, but he had thought that apart from the royal family, no one actually lived in such a fortress. They left the cab at the foot of a stone staircase and mounted the steps; a woman slightly younger than Beard, and far more expensively attired, met them at a massive carved wooden door.

"Wills, I am so very glad to see you," said the Duchess, smiling broadly with well-aligned if yellowed teeth. "I have a volume of poetry for you that I know you will like."

"Thank you, Your Grace. The young gentleman is Mr. Newman, from America."

Bucky extended his hand, but the Duchess merely inclined her head. "How good of you to visit."

They stepped into a cavernous foyer so grand that it appeared one of the largest rooms in the estate had been pushed to the front. The endless sweep of marble flooring was broken only by two round stone tables, topped by decorative urns overflowing with lilies and sprigs of greenery. Something about the flowers was off, and Bucky moved to pass with arm's reach of the nearest urn. The blooms were silk.

"I've seen documentaries about places like this. There must be an amazing backstory."

"Indeed there is," the Duchess replied. "Allow me to show you." She ushered them through a doorway and into a salon of prodigious dimensions; along three of the four walls, floor-to-ceiling vitrines presented her collection of porcelain figures: cockerels and goldfinches, parrots, peacocks, Scaramouche and Columbine, Europa and the Bull. The furniture was a mix of antique English settees and Chinese lacquer cabinets on stands. In a bay window stood a magnificent double-keyboard Broadwood harpsichord, apparently in working condition.

"Do you play?" Bucky asked.

The Duchess laughed as if the very idea were absurd. "Not a note! But we always have period music at my parties."

The adjacent dining room boasted built-in sideboards and seating for twenty-four, but each of the carved mahogany chairs had a sharp-scaled pine cone placed at the center of its embroidered seat, a clear warning to any unwelcome derrières. They passed through a library filled with richly bound books, where two volumes of *The Baronial Halls of England* lay upon a side table, and then into a final room of astonishing length, apparently running the entire width of the house. Even more remarkable was the palette—the walls had been painted a brilliant pink, with crown molding in fuchsia.

"I hope you find the redecoration pleasing, the color choices are mine. The Long Gallery had been a faded green since before my husband passed, and this is so much more enervating."

"You mean eye-catching, Your Grace," Beard corrected.

The Duchess directed Bucky's attention to a contemporary portrait at the head of the room, the only work rendered in water-soluble crayon. "This was my late husband, the ninth Duke. He was a dear man, but impractical in his tastes, as you can tell from the scale of this property. I'm afraid it was a fetal flaw in his character. Still, one can forgive him for wanting to keep Westerley Park; after all, the estate was granted to my husband's ancestor by the King."

"When was that?"

"Oh, a long time ago. You must realize, we had the most frightful civil war in England; the very best people lost their titles, and nearly as important from a family perspective, their heads. My husband's ancestors were Royalists, so when Charles I went to the block, a number of them met with equally unpleasant ends." She motioned to a much older portrait on one of the long side walls—a man on horseback with Van Dyke whiskers—as behind her, Beard drew a finger across his throat.

The Duchess called his attention to another portrait of a royal with flowing curls and oily skin, resplendent in layers of lace and blue silk. "Here is the great benefactor of our family, Charles II. He elevated my late husband's ancestor to nobility when the monarchy was restored, after the Interruptus."

"You mean the Interregnum, Your Grace," Beard said more firmly.

"Yes, yes, all right, Wills. At any rate, the land for Westerley Park was deeded to the family at that time, and the manor and other structures were added over the generations that followed. Naturally, after the last war it became much more difficult to keep up a place like this, and before he died, my husband expressed his idea to give the estate to the National Trust. But I said, 'No, dear, I shall find a way to keep it in the family,' and so I have. We host weddings, bar mitzvahs, memorial services, and corporate functions, and in what were once the stables we have a full catering operation."

"Smart play," said Bucky. "You have to do whatever it takes to stay in the game."

"But speaking of monarchs reminds me of the book I have for you, Wills." The Duchess led them out of the Long Gallery and back into the paneled library.

"I was recently introduced to a gifted poet by the name of Philo Creacher," she explained, retrieving a slim paperback from the shelves. "He's just published a tribute to Edward VII, written entirely in rhyming verse. The way he captures Edward's affairs with the French theater set is so romantic. Here, let me read you a few lines." She opened the volume, raised it up, and thrust out a fleshy arm like an orator—

> *Each time these stirrings arose in his pants,*
> *Brave Edward would hasten to Paris, France*
> *Thespian beauties beloved of the stage,*
> *Vied to caress the great man of the age*
> *To the stirring blare of his royal trumpets,*
> *He'd mount and master the Gallic strumpets,*
> *Our monarch's belly then flopped and jiggled,*
> *As beneath his great bulk they gamely wriggled…*

You see what I mean, Wills, it's a tower de force, and the summit of poetisy!" She handed him the book as a gift.

"I shall treasure it always, Your Grace. It will have a special place on my nightstand."

Bucky couldn't be certain, but he thought that after "night-stand" the Duchess winked at Beard. Like the phony flowers in the entry hall, something about "Her Grace" was less than real; her gestures were too broad, her linguistic flubs too numerous, her manner more like an actress trying to *play* a duchess than the genuine blue-blooded article. And an obvious question loomed: what was Beard's connection to this eccentric aristocrat?

He wouldn't find out on the spot. The Duchess herded them forward through the yawning house, past drawing rooms and antechambers to a sunlit conservatory where a young woman in servant's attire brought them white wine and bowls of mixed berries, and a three-tiered silver tray of finger sandwiches with the crusts removed. After Beard's surprise wake-up call, Bucky had not had time for breakfast; suddenly feeling his hunger, he chewed ravenously through all the food, sloshing it down with *Pouilly-Fuissé.*

"I am pleased that you enjoy our cuisine, Mr. Newman. But you didn't mention what brought you to England."

Bucky reminded himself to swallow before answering. "I'm working with a partner to launch a gentlemen's club in London. Will drove me to the location yesterday for an initial assessment of our facility."

"Isn't he just the most capable driver you have ever known? So tell me, what is the location you have chosen?"

"Belgrave Square. It sets the right tone for the clientele we hope to attract."

"How marvelous! I knew immediately that you were a young man of excellent taste. You must advise me when you open your portals, so that I may refer exceptional members."

As their visit with the Duchess ended, Bucky's head was spinning with French wine and English warfare. He was still trying to sort out the two Charleses, Edward some-number-or-other, and precisely whose neck had been bifurcated. Before entering the mansion he had silenced his phone, and now, back in Beard's cab, he checked to see if Dayna had responded to his latest message—the amazing news about his new contract and the massive cash infusion. He yearned to hear her recant her spiteful text from the day of his firing. Hadn't he proved he could recover with astonishing speed? That he would make good on every promise and commitment? And though he wouldn't rub it in, exactly, he intended to make the point that she should never doubt him again. The messages icon showed nothing new since the morning, but as he considered why, he received two live calls a moment apart. The first was Yuri; he sent it to voice mail. With joy and relief he saw that the second caller was Dayna.

"Hey, I thought I'd never reach you!" he said with just a hint of reproach. "You didn't think I'd be on the sidelines for long, did you? Listen, the new gig is amazing, it's way better than—"

"Wait, Bucky, I have something important to say to you."

"So you won't believe this, I just had lunch with a duchess. But don't be jealous, she's twice your age and her teeth are yellower than your mother's. We're leaving her estate right now… it looks like Carnegie's castle on steroids."

"Bucky," she cut in, "*BUCKY!*"

"Take it easy, I hear you."

"No you don't. You aren't even listening. I'm sorry, but this isn't going to work."

"Babe, what do you mean? It's all good. I've got money for your flight, and we can look for a flat as soon as you get here. It'll be awesome, I promise."

"Whatever you're doing now, I'm sure it's *formidable*, but people in Manhattan are still furious about what happened. They're not going to give me a job in London just so I can be with you. And I have my own reputation to think about."

"So being my girlfriend puts the stink on you at work?"

She paused for a long time before answering. "Oh, Bucky… Daddy always said you were no *chevalier* in shining armor." Then she was gone.

He tried to hold it together, sucking in slow, agonized breaths, on the verge of cutting loose a shriek but determined not to break down in Beard's hack. He had been Dayna's lover for more than two years—long enough to picture the house and the kids and the Irish setter, and think happily about sleeping together for the rest of their lives. Instead she had kicked him to the curb with a thirty-second call. He faked a cough to hide his sob.

On his phone, a tiny "1" appeared at the corner of the calls icon—Yuri had hung up. Still in shock, he retrieved the message instinctively. He had expected that a week or two, even a month, might pass before any real work began, but now came news that his Russian partner had marshaled his resources in haste. Incredibly, the tear-out phase had already begun at the Belgrave Square house.

"We must discuss ensuing steps," Yuri said briskly. "There is much for you to do, *tovarish*."

FIVE

Over the weeks that followed, an evolving army of east European tradesmen appeared each morning at the house. Gangs of reeking tear-out workers gave way to framers and floor men, plumbers and electricians, masons, finish carpenters, lathe and plaster specialists, tile artists, and interior painters, all crashing past the enameled entry door and tumbling over each other in a welter of Slavic cries and curses. Above them, from a balustrade overlooking the great entry hall, Yuri Dolgorukov directed like an orchestra conductor. As if from a wave of his baton, a carpentry shop and supply dump had sprung up in a whirl of noise and sawdust, where screeching table saws and rasping planes and routers fought to drown out the nail guns and power drills. Heaps of lumber, plaster, stone, and wire had been pushed up high in every corner, with Yuri overseeing each delivery of material, dispatching windows and doors, chandeliers, carpets, marble slabs, and rich hardwood veneers to their proper places in his intricate plan.

And he was building down as well as up. Daily his crew burrowed deeper into the ground beneath the property, excavating a cavernous space. A conveyor belt at the rear of the house brought up tons of chunky clay, which was shoveled onto trucks and carted off. He explained, "Certain pleasures are best enjoyed discreetly. I build special playroom below street level for naughtiest boys."

Bucky had checked out of his hotel and moved to Belgrave Square as soon as work began, joining Yuri, who had already taken up residence. They now inhabited two bedrooms and a connecting workroom at the rear of the ground floor. Yuri's plan called for these rooms to become their private offices once the club was complete, but Bucky wasn't waiting—as his partner had correctly stated, there was much for him to do. Still rocked by the breakup with Dayna, he tried to fill every waking moment with activities that would mask his pain. First, with the help of a pricey solicitor, he created a chain of dummy entities to paper over their true plans. Speeds & Feeds, LLC was duly registered in Bermuda, and within it a wholly-owned subsidiary in the Pitcairn Islands, called Nebula Corp. This firm, in turn, controlled a revocable trust in Gibraltar, and the trust listed as an asset a Guernsey-based import-export company, International Fulfillment, Ltd. That company's first official act was to issue a new work permit, allowing him to remain in the country. After the solicitor swore that no court on earth could ever crack open the Russian doll series and seize the sheltered funds, Bucky opened a bank account for International Fulfillment. The next day the account balance surged, as the oligarch's ante for remodeling expenses arrived by wire transfer from a numbered account in Dubai.

With work underway, dozens of bills flooded Bucky's in-basket, seeking payment for materials, skilled labor, delivery charges, and mysterious items like "council taxes." And each day brought new bothers, from permits and licenses to building inspections to palms outstretched in want of grease. To organize purchasing, he created a master list of basic needs: baccarat, blackjack, and poker tables; a craps table and a roulette wheel; dice sticks and roulette rakes; dealer shoes and cases of playing cards, betting chips, and colorful dice; icemakers, dishwashers, beverage coolers, and coffee machines; glasses and barware, serving ware and silverware; beer, ale, wine, whisky, gin, vodka, rum, tequila, and ninety-four types of liqueurs and mixers; towels, sheets, pillows, and duvets; condoms, lube, vibrating toys, Ben Wa balls and horse-tailed butt plugs; grocery service, garbage service, linen service, newspaper service, and a sworn-to-silence maid service.

But all of this counted for nothing compared to the well-spring of true success. He began an online search for what Yuri had called "tasteful women." From the day he arrived in London, it had seemed to him that through architectural sleight of hand, the city hoodwinked visitors into believing it was a staid metropolis. But virtual London was a carnival blowout of digital flesh, cavorting across his laptop screen and dancing on the lighted stage of his phone. He clicked through page after page of Hungarian blondes, Romanian redheads, leather-clad Austrians, and elfin Asians amenable to "A and O levels," all touting their availability in Mayfair, Knightsbridge, Notting Hill, Soho, or Sloane Square. He had assumed that perhaps a few dozen escorts would have created profile pages or stand-alone websites to ply their trade, but he was off by several powers of ten. In two days he bookmarked thousands of pleasure sites, many boasting scores of girls, with photo galleries, details on their services and rates, even blunt testimonials to their skills and charms submitted by sated punters. But would any of these women be proper companions for the wildly rich?

He decided to automate the sorting process with a targeted search bot and a script that scored the returns. His algorithm gave points to girls who spoke multiple languages, or were published models who had achieved high fees in their work, and deducted points from those who were too young, too inexperienced, or too restrictive in their services. He deciphered the catalogue of acronyms for favored sexual practices, and built into his sorting code a scale of values for GFE, OWO, CIM, and the other winking euphemisms, then turned the bot loose on a geographically limited zone. In minutes he had his answer: there were 27,612 tarts in the south of England. Fewer than 1 percent merited a closer look. His goal was to hire the best of the lot—multilingual hedonists with drop-dead looks—but the path to meeting them wasn't clear. How could he hope for contact unless he pretended to be a punter? And with the house unfinished, where would he conduct the interviews? He noticed that all the escorts had different in-call and outcall rates; the cost was greater if you wanted the girl to turn up at your hotel room. That sparked an idea. He counted out his remaining cash—plenty for two nights in a suite at the Ritz.

The following afternoon he strode up Piccadilly and into the hotel's domed lobby in an unaccustomed tie and jacket, to comply with the stuffy dress code. He was shown to an upper-floor suite with glass doors that opened onto stunning views of Green Park. Ornately woven carpets of blue, burgundy, and gold softened the floors of the lounge and bedchamber; the expansive rooms glittered with dark Empire furniture, the gilded accents matching the trim on the white walls and doors. He had chosen an attractive French brunette, Marie-Chantal, as his first appointment, one of a parade of candidates whom he intended to interview that evening. He ordered champagne and tea sandwiches, which came up with lightning speed on a rolling cart, and sensing that he might need the strength, he fortified himself with two of the little morsels, one egg-mayonnaise and another that tasted like salmon. When she arrived, Marie-Chantal looked older, broader in the hips, and more dependent on makeup than the photographs he remembered, and her accent was not French, but something closer to Ukrainian.

"You're a young one, aren't you?" she said with a sly laugh. "I haven't had one your age since my second or third year in London."

"How long have you lived here?"

"Long enough to know my way around. Is that champagne for me?"

Bucky poured a glass for each of them and asked her to join him in the sitting room. "I should clarify that I'm not planning to have sex with you."

A harsher expression darkened Marie-Chantal's face. "Are you a police officer?"

"No, just the opposite," he said, instantly regretting his diction. "What I mean to say—"

"I hope you understand you still have to pay me."

"Absolutely, I intend to." He handed her enough cash for an hour's work, and watched it disappear into an alligator purse, clenched tightly at her side.

"Do you want fetish, then? Unless it's something disgusting, I might be willing to accommodate."

Bucky swallowed half the glass of champagne at a toss, and stifled a belch. "My business partner and I are opening a private gentlemen's club in one of the best parts of London. We're looking for the most talented girls, to cater to high-end customers. You could still work outcalls, but the club will be spectacular and draw a stream of affluent men."

"You? You are going to do *this*?" She began to laugh in a string of high-pitched whoops, slapping her hands on her ample thighs and rocking forward and back on the settee. "So tell me, Don Juan, what would be the splits?"

"I'm sorry?"

"You don't even know what that means, do you? On out-calls through a service any girl who can get past the doorman keeps fifty percent of the fee, and the entire tip. For in-calls at a house, it's forty to the girl and sixty for the house. But I book my own business and keep every penny, so there's nothing more to talk about. Thank you for the very cold champagne, and I wish you the most tremendous success, once you learn anything at all about this business." She went out clutching her bag, but before the door slammed behind her, Bucky heard her sneer, "Wanker!" in the hallway.

Staggered by his own ignorance, he went to work on the numbers. The splits suggested an obvious tactic. Every trading firm in Manhattan would negotiate one-off commission sharing deals with serious rainmakers. Suppose he bumped the splits to fifty-fifty at the house, and offered the girls two-thirds of the revenue on outcalls? With that as a hook, could they poach the prettiest talent from local rivals, and maybe acquire some high-rolling "regulars" in the process? They might even be able to make up the loss by charging more; he had seen the rich pay outlandish sums for art and wine and collector cars deemed to be the finest, so why wouldn't they pony up for the cream of the courtesans? It was worth trying. And just in time, as the next knock at the door delivered Isabella, a short, busty, charming Italian, with a musical laugh that rang through the suite. In addition to her own language and English, she spoke French, German, and Spanish. "Everything good starts with my mouth," she said, her dark eyes twinkling.

"This isn't what you came here expecting, but I'm not a cop, and what I'm going to offer you may be more than you're making now." Bucky outlined his improved splits, and asked if she might be interested.

Isabella was, along with five of thirteen other girls who arrived punctually at half-hour intervals. At midnight he descended to the lobby, hoping the dining room would still be open. The concierge pointed the way, then touched his arm. "You're the gentleman in the Trafalgar Suite, aren't you, sir? Can you tell me what pills a man needs to take, to shag as many women as you have this evening?"

When the selection was complete he arranged for Yuri to

meet the girls; they appeared punctually at the Belgrave Square house after the workers had left for the day. He led them to a salon off the entry hall, briefly swept clear of construction debris and staged with crystal glasses, liquor, and wine on ice. Charlotte, a sometime singer from Norwich, and Amanda, a fetching actress from the East End, were the only Brits; his choice had also fallen on Ruta, a Latvian glamour model with translucent hair, and Kanokwan, from Phuket, who explained that among other delights, she gave full-body Thai massages— using her *full* body. In the house she would become "Kandy." From Circus Sophia came Krassy and Sassy, twin Bulgarian acrobats whose expertise spanned hot oil wrestling and *ménage à trois*. And along with the ever-laughing Isabella, Bucky had picked Linnea from the corps de ballet of Oslo, the marvelously tattooed Kimiko from Osaka, and Mandy, an Australian surfer with a perfect tan and dazzling teeth.

But even amid this galaxy of beauties, one of the girls stood apart, towering over them in Louboutin heels. A Brazilian blend of black, brown, and tan, Fabiana was wonderfully tall with toned limbs and a spilling waterfall of hair. She appeared to have spent every day of her life playing beach volleyball, and every night on the dance floor. Yuri's eyes bulged when she stood before him, the only one of the girls he was forced to look up to. He attempted to converse with her, but what came out was gibberish.

Fabiana stroked his arm. "We will be close, I feel this already."

When they had gone, Yuri beamed his pleasure. "Fantastic girls, I am desirous of the Brazilian! But where are domme and sub?" Bucky regarded him blankly. Then Yuri explained the rich opportunity at the extremes of the pleasure gamut, and the need to offer their members the chance to play master or slave, according to their fantasies.

In the morning Bucky went to work on these unantici-
pated requests, hoping to secure what they required over the
telephone, without the expense of more nights at the Ritz. At
midafternoon, a fresh-faced English girl in a school jumper
and a blonde ponytail bounced into the house, at first glance
appearing to be no more than a teenager. He started in alarm—
an underage girl could bring the law down on their heads. But
as she began to speak, his fear evaporated.

"I am Knotty Natalie," she said in a polished Cambridge
accent. "I love ornamental and predicament bondage, suspension play, and caging. I can take the slipper, tawse, and cane to
medium-heavy levels, and any amount of spanking, whether
bound or over the knee. I am also an experienced role-player,
and I have an extensive wardrobe including a French maid's
costume, prison clothing, and proper uniform for a Navy Wren."

"You're well-spoken. How far did you get in school?"

"Actually, I'm in the second year of a PhD program."

"I didn't know they awarded doctoral degrees in bondage
and discipline."

"This being Britain, you might be surprised," Natalie
said wryly. "But since you ask, my dissertation concerns the
electro-chemistry of neurotransmission across the synapse.
This is my way of graduating with a paid-off flat and a savings
account."

A bigger bombshell fell that evening. Hours after dark,
Bucky dozed in a chair, his stomach stuffed with lamb. He
awoke to knocking at the front door, but before he could get
up, Yuri greeted the caller. He heard a low, distinctive female
voice in the entry hall, then the door swept open and an image
came thrusting into the room like a bayonet. In the first instant
there was a hard quality to the woman's face, but in the next
it became striking, then with another step, powerfully lovely.
Her hair was so intensely black that it flashed a hint of gun

bluing, and her movements revealed a swimmer's hips and an abdomen taut as carbon fiber. As she advanced he was suddenly enveloped in a Chanel cloud, delicious in his nostrils, then he was on his feet without knowing why.

"You sounded taller on the phone," the visitor said with a dark South African inflection. She paused for his response but he was dumbstruck. "I can't imagine I'm the first one who's ever told you that? No matter. My proper name is Angelica Smuts, but my clients know me as Mistress von Adder." She handed him a black business card with the motto "None shall 'scape whipping."

"And your specialty?"

"Bollocking and the lash."

"Jesus wept!"

"Believe me, he would if I had been there."

Yuri appeared at the door. "Dungeon is unfinished, but perhaps you wish to show our guest the ample dimensions of lower level?"

Bucky had paid little attention to the underground play-room; he hadn't bothered to check on its progress for weeks. At Yuri's urging he led the way down the cellar staircase, his hand sweeping the wall for a light switch. He found it at the bottom step, but strangely, only pale illumination filtered down from the purplish bulbs scattered above their heads. Sheets of black leatherette covered the walls of the oblong dungeon, and a padded carpet deadened every footfall. Moving forward warily he discovered an array of metal pulleys and eyebolts secured to the ceiling joists, and at the far end, an oversize doghouse constructed of aluminum bars. A tangled heap of riding crops, floggers, and braided whips lay beside the cage.

"Well, I suppose it's a start," Angelica said critically. "You'll need a St. Andrew's Cross, pillory, motorized hoist, whipping benches, and wall racks for at least one hundred implements.

See what you can find in red patent leather to add a splash of color, and if you could manage some lounge furniture in black and a bed of nails with locking wrist and ankle cuffs, it wouldn't hurt."

"I'll look into it," Bucky said, trying to process the implications of her requests. "So do you just beat them half to death?"

"Don't be ridiculous, do you think I have no skill at all? It could just as easily be a tie-and-tease or a mind fuck, or one of my obedience rituals. Not everyone responds to pain, some men can be broken more easily through the denial of pleasure. But I promise you, I do break them all, one way or another."

The odd thing was that each razor remark made Angelica Smuts more charismatic; the war between her dark nature and her arresting physical beauty threw off a witchy energy. Her Boer accent was the icing on the cake. A lesser woman would never have dared to speak and act as she did, but to Bucky, it explained why men would pay to experience her wrath. The following morning his first waking thought was of Angelica—she had managed to invade his subconscious, though he couldn't remember dreaming about her. He lay in bed, eyes closed, picturing her dominating and abusing some trussed-up perv. There was nothing remotely appealing about the image, and yet somehow Angelica fascinated him.

■ ■ ■

The sense of progress grew daily, and with the girls standing ready, Bucky began to consider how to promote the club. Yuri had left it to him to choose a name, and he considered the most obvious choices: *The Belgravia Club*, *The Millennium Club*, or maybe a single word like *Monarchs* or *Premiers*. They all seemed equally trite. But after mocking up a simple website, using the name from the import-export firm as a placeholder, he found himself liking International Fulfillment. It was vague enough to be seen as harmless by the outside world, but their initiated members would read beyond the moniker and into the metaphor. That still left him with a PR problem: the true nature of their enterprise could never be revealed on the web. He had to find another way to get the word out. He had heard nothing from Dayna since their breakup; his multiple calls rolled to voice mail, and his texts confirming the wire transfers for half their New York rent drew no acknowledgment. It occurred to him that asking for professional advice would be a credible excuse to contact her. He sent an e-mail, explaining that he was developing a specialty business for an elite clientele—the profile was high-net-worth males over thirty. Their public website could offer only platitudes, and print and broadcast media were off the table. What else might she suggest to drive business growth?

He hoped that along with any practical suggestions, she would ask how he was getting on, even open the door to renewed communications. But the next morning brought a cool response. *I recommend optimizing your paradigm for UK revenue enhancement by leveraging only appropriate modalities, especially affiliate marketing and social networking. Best practices call for integrating marketing automation with your CRM platform, and deployment of a cloud-based ERP suite. Above all else, be true to your Brand Values.*

He sent back a blank reply with a one-word subject line, *Merci.* Angelica Smuts had been correct, there were countless ways to torture a man.

That evening Yuri came to him with a different problem. "In our business, cash will always be stolen, as banknotes pass between the sheets. We must find a more intelligent way to collect what is owed."

Bucky was stumped, knowing that men of great wealth

often carried no wallet. Then he remembered something that Yuri had said, that first night in the pub in Tottenham, asking if he could "make website and mobile app." He had an inspiration—they would run the club off smartphones and tablets. In days of furious round-the-clock coding he developed an app that handled it all: initiation fees and annual renewals, cocktails and casino chips, private dinners, spa services, Cuban cigars, and all their tempting specialties. Every pleasure and possibility would appear at the touch of intuitive menus; bartenders could track multiple tabs, and croupiers dispense any sum in chips, then offer members a screen for a fingertip signature. But the part he looked upon with pride was the sub-app for the girls, with their personal rates for every kind of kink and romp. As each liaison reached its climax, the satisfied member would sign with a flourish and the bill and tip would credit to the house's back-end system. All of it—food and drink, gambling and sex, every purchase and indulgence—would roll up to the members' monthly statements and be billed to their credit cards.

When he showed the beta version to Yuri, his partner's eyes filled with tears. "You are genius, Bucky, genius!"

Midway through the implementation he had an unnerving insight—prospective members would call and size up the club based on the vocal qualities of their first contact. Someone needed to field those calls, and that person could not be a man, or an American. He had lived in London long enough to experience the variety of British accents, and his first thought was to hire an English major straight out of Oxford. But that led to a stickier problem. When members wanted to book time with their favorite girls, or ask about something more adventurous, most would simply telephone. The club's phone rep would need to discuss every possible act without shame, and deftly segue to dates, times, and prices, then convert the appointments. He posted an online ad and called back twenty-seven applicants before discovering Laira, a fortyish woman from Bournemouth who had recently moved to London. Her satin voice was clear, intelligent, disarming, and utterly English.

"I've had six boyfriends, two husbands, and three children," Laira confided. "I doubt that any of your callers will succeed in putting me off with their shocking desires."

Now that the heavy carpentry and stonework of the early stages were complete, and finish work underway, Yuri turned his attention to the subtleties. Among the many refinements was his management of acoustics; he explained that the dungeon and their offices were soundproofed, and stereo loudspeakers had been installed in every bedroom. When the system was ready, Yuri revealed his musical tastes. To Bucky's surprise his partner came out as a classical music buff, though his preference wasn't the fluffy favorites—Tchaikovsky, Rimsky-Korsakov, Rachmaninoff—but discordant, percussive works by Prokofiev and Shostakovich. His special favorite was the march from *The Love for Three Oranges,* which echoed through the house as Yuri goose-stepped to the martial rhythms. Unfortunately, modern composers were not the only source of dissonance. Bucky returned one afternoon from his latest round of errands to find Yuri in the lower salon, speaking in hushed tones with an imposing older gentleman. Two hired-muscle types lurked behind the visitor.

"Ah, Bucky, I have pleasure to introduce you to our illustrious benefactor, Nicolai Vasilievitch Klepakov."

So here was the great man. The oligarch wore a beautifully tailored cashmere topcoat with a collar of mink; wisps of smoke from a brown cigarette clouded his graying head and sloping shoulders, polluting the salon with the odors of mule dung and toluene.

Bucky stuck out his hand. "It's an honor to meet you." But

Klepakov would not suffer to speak to him directly; he turned away, holding out a limp palm so that Bucky could only grasp a few pudgy fingers and tug at them awkwardly. As soon as he let go, the Boss moved to a pile of framed canvases lying loose in a window bay, flipping through them casually, muttering, "Caillebotte, Cassatt, Manet, Morisot, Pissarro⊠" He paused for a lovely work in oils, whose palette ideally accented the salon: "*Da*, Sisley!" He handed the painting to one of his skulking henchmen, who tucked it under his arm, then went out without speaking again, after pausing to reach into his pants and shake his personal organs into place.

Bucky wasn't sure if the oligarch's visit had aroused their curiosity, but soon after, he noticed that each time he left the house, he was watched from the embassy next door. Twice, as he waited at the curb for Will Beard to collect him for an errand run, he turned to see curtains quickly drawn shut in an upper window of the German mission. It amused him to think how little they could learn from their remote vantage point; had they been able to spy into the club's interior rooms, they would likely have concluded it was a movie set for a historical drama. Bucky had grown up in a sticks-and-bricks tract home, with his half-dozen siblings stacked high in rickety bunk beds. Crown moldings and mahogany doors could only be Hollywood props, never mind decorative plasterwork or a gilded frieze that reproduced the patterns from the Temple of Venus. Beyond this excess, Yuri had actually given names to his favorite chambers. The main lounge and gaming floor was not "the casino" or "the bar" but the Grand Saloon, adjoined by a fan-ventilated Tobacco Room and the purplish Velvet Drawing Room, a waiting area for members soon to experience the delights of the bedrooms. The third floor offered Hadrian's Baths—a suite of saunas and massage stalls—and for the bookishly inclined, the ground level boasted a London extension of the Library of Ephesus.

Not my first mansion, Yuri had boasted, and clearly there was more to come.

As the weeks progressed, the frantic pace of their work began to tell. Bucky suffered a spate of mental errors, then irritability, and finally a need to sleep twelve hours at a stretch. He had experienced these symptoms before, at college, and knew the best cure was a liquored-up road trip. But this time he wanted to mix discovery with drunkenness. The challenges of the Belgravia project often reminded him of the hero engineers that Will Beard had mentioned, that first day in his cab. He was curious to see—from his twenty-first century perspective—what I. K. Brunel and Max Newman had achieved in the nineteenth and twentieth centuries. Brunel's railway projects suggested a route, which could include a trip to Bletchley Park on the return to London. He traveled by train to Maidenhead, where he viewed Brunel's celebrated bridge, then did without supper and drank until he was reeling. He had almost forgotten what it was like to go to bars without a girlfriend to hold him back—to have no reason on earth to pull up short of unconsciousness. His stupor was glorious. A day later he was on to Chippenham, where he inspected Brunel's viaducts, and he traversed the darkly miraculous Box Tunnel before staying over in Bath. Once again he crawled from pub to tavern, wetting down walls in lonely alleys. At Bristol he disembarked at Temple Meads Station, intending to look it over before taking in the steamship that Beard had mentioned, Brunel's *SS Great Britain*. But his tour of the remarkable vessel was pushed back a day, in favor of more time with a glass in his hand.

A day later he reversed course, journeying beyond Oxford to Milton Keynes, then down to Bletchley Park. He explored the rambling main house and the tiny post office, the maritime display and the Churchill memorabilia, before viewing what he had really come to see. Like a space film fantasy, the rebuilt

Colossus blinked and buzzed, its switches clacking loudly as it churned through permutations. The rows of bulbs and buttons only hinted at generations of machines to come, the cluster of wheels for the paper tape looking more like a Dobby loom than a modern computer. Yet Beard had been correct. With this ungainly device—the brainchild of the Newmanry section—Hitler's highest-security messages had been deciphered. For a moment his fascination with technology came roaring back, the force that had driven his life for a decade, until he imagined Max Newman standing before him, demanding an account. *Well then, Bucky my lad, what have you accomplished?*

He had left for three days and come back in six, his liver crying out for mercy but his mind refreshed. When he returned late in the evening no change was apparent from the street; he unlocked the front door expecting to see the house still blanketed in dust and strewn with scraps of wood and wire, its rooms empty of furnishings. But the great black panel swung open to a changed world. He stepped into a space that had been scrubbed and polished and artfully decorated, and he felt the personality of the club spring flamboyantly to life.

His eyes were drawn at once from the parquet floor of the Entry Hall up the length of fluted half columns to a marble colonnade, and soaring high above, a coffered ceiling of intricate beauty. In trompe-l'oeil scenes on the plaster walls, nymphs and satyrs frolicked and fornicated across the Elysian fields. At the center points of the walls, the colonnade was interrupted by huge bronze-over-plaster medallions honoring Cupid, Venus, Bacchus, and, below the open Grand Saloon, Hymen, god of marriage. Alongside the stairs, almost as an afterthought, Yuri had arranged a collection of multi-hued codpieces on a Chippendale credenza.

Bucky mounted the superb staircase, caressing the carved mahogany pineapple atop the first newel post; at the landing, the Saloon extended to the rear of the house, its walls rich with block paneled walnut. Gaming tables had been loosely arranged to encourage members to drift and play, and then to visit the imposing padauk-wood bar with its gleaming counter. Behind the bar, bottled spirits dazzled in the ceiling-height mirrors, fronted by hanging racks of crystal ware.

Wandering from floor to floor, he realized that Yuri's most inspired artistry had been lavished on the bedrooms, which emerged as flights of fantasy—sexual as well as architectural. The Adventurer's Bedroom sported a Crusader's cape beneath a pair of curving Saracen sabers, a set of crossed halberds, a brace of French double-barreled dueling pistols, and an elaborately inlaid flintlock musketoon. Tiger and zebra skins crouched on the floors of the Hunter's Bedroom, the walls and tables fitted out with Masai and Matabele shields, a Renaissance hunting horn, and an oil of St. George slaying a dragon with a lengthy spear. The Classical Bedroom offered Etruscan urns with erotic themes, a Greek hoplite helmet, and a framed copy of Poussin's *Abduction of the Sabine Women.* Each of the eleven working bedrooms boasted its own fireplace, with heavy pewter fireboxes and gleaming fenders; over the fireplaces, mantles of sculpted Cararra marble were accented by matching chinoiserie. Throughout the bedrooms, chestnut, wenge, cocobolo and pearwood had been trimmed and shaped into bookcases, window seats, or banks of cabinets, and every wall had been perfected with wainscoting and ornate window casements, beneath sumptuous ceilings that danced with plaster embellishments. While he had crawled the pubs of Bristol, Yuri had taken delivery of van-loads of furniture, books, and art. Now the glass-fronted cases in the Library bulged with titles ranging from Halsbury's *Laws of England* to Cleland's *Memoirs of a Woman of Pleasure,* and every room was fitted out with great oak armoires, delicate writing tables, oil portraits and watercolor landscapes, even a grandfather clock in the Entry Hall that rang the hours in a baritone voice.

In a breathless moment Bucky saw that he had overestimated St. Paul's Cathedral and even the Palace of Westminster. Their Belgrave Square bordello was the real triumph of British architecture.

It still troubled him that the Germans kept watch from their upper windows, but as the time approached to hang out a sign, he hoped the club's ambiguous name would mollify their neighbors. From a specialties shop in Fulham he ordered a rectangular door plaque of heavy polished brass, with matching mounting screws. On the afternoon the club opened for business, he secured the plaque to the front door and rubbed the brass finish until it gleamed, highlighting the embossed black letters. He stood back on the sidewalk, filled with pride and awareness of the distance they had covered, as he admired their new identity—

INTERNATIONAL
FULFILLMENT

SIX

Bucky figured the real trick of their first weeks in business would be navigating the float—croupiers, cooks, bartenders, and maids expected regular paychecks, and the girls required cash on delivery, while members' bills cleared only at the end of the month. But the first crisis came when a Swedish rummy needed throwing out. The Stockholm shipping magnate hurled a drink in the face of a car maker from Seoul and dared him to try out his tae kwon do; wisely, the flyweight barman wanted no part of any fisticuffs. Bucky raced up from the office and manhandled Herr Håkansson to the top of the stairs, but their feet tangled and they tumbled down to the first landing, where with luck the troublemaker promptly went to sleep. With the help of Krassy and Sassy, the strongest of the girls, he lugged the portly Swede to the alley and propped him against a rubbish bin.

The following day he posted an opening for a bouncer on three online jobs boards, then went out for curry. He returned to find that a mob of hooligans had laid siege to the house, stamping and spitting and threatening bloody mayhem unless they were seen at once about the job. Each of the monsters was marked by a different deformity—cauliflower ears, a pushed-over nose, juiced-up arms and shoulders—and all wore black leather coats and baggy pants as if this were the standard uniform for punch-up duty. Bucky lowered his face into his jacket and crept around the back, entering the house through the alley.

Yuri was waiting. "Why you put on fucking Internet? I have trusted man, recommended by nightclub owner."

An enormous bull stepped forward, his scalp bristling with spiky hair like shards atop a barrier wall. "I'm Jackie Wax, guv'nor. I'd be interested in the bouncing job. I mix drinks too, if that's anything what helps you out."

Bucky gaped at his pumpkin head and barrel chest. Wax was a foot taller and more than twice his own weight; his paws were borrowed from a polar bear. "The barman on duty last night wasn't much use to us when it hit the fan."

Wax let out a little chuckle. "If there's one thing I know, guv'nor, it's how to deal with any man what can't hold his liquor."

"Fine. If you get rid of those hoodlums outside the front door, the job is yours."

"It's done, guv'nor." He strode to the entry, threw back the door and punched the closest man squarely in the nose. A ferocious brouhaha erupted on the steps, as Wax pressed forward leveling thug after goon with a hail of thunderous clouts.

"You see, he is admirable bouncer," Yuri cried. He peered through the open doorway, positioning Bucky as a shield against the melee. His chosen man was wasting no time—molars flew and ribs cracked as clobbered louts collapsed to the sidewalk.

Wax quickly battered his way clear into the street. By twos and threes the yobs came at him, flailing wildly, cursing and clawing, all their punches missing as he sent them bloodied to the pavement. "Here's for your bollocks, mate!" he roared, flattening the last pretender with a god-awful boot to the groin. He looked about in satisfaction as the scene became quiet. A dozen unconscious forms littered the pavement.

Bucky pointed toward the grassy square. "Could you drag

them into the park?"

"Not to worry, guv'nor. I'll sprinkle 'em with a bit of whisky in case a copper should happen by."

When he returned they settled the matter of pay, while Yuri advised the pacifist barman that his services were no longer required.

Wax pulled Bucky aside for a private word. "I hear you had a go at throwin' one out yerself? That won't be needed when I'm around, but I can't work seven days or all hours. I have a wife and two daughters, and God knows why, but they like to see me now and then. So here's some advice. If you ever need to put a man down, yer best chance is to stomp on his foot. It's the last move he'll expect, and it hurts like flamin' hell. When he hollers you knock his teeth out."

"Where did you learn that?"

"In the Parachute Regiment."

Thankfully, other shocks were peaceable. Relying chiefly on a whisper campaign and the oligarch's connections to spread the word about the club, Bucky anticipated a slow ramp-up to profitability. By opening day, just seven charter members had put up the £9,900 initiation fee. But as these early adopters discovered the true meaning of International Fulfillment, the name acquired a more compelling resonance. After two weeks the club had forty members; at month's end nearly one hundred. Bucky's greater dread was the emergence of another Marie-Chantal, hard as flint and quick to anger, and Yuri warned him to beware of drugs and drunken tantrums, and hair-pulling catfights over the girls' much-prized regulars. Hoping it would head off the most predictable dispute, he made a habit of paying them all without delay. But to his immense relief, the stereotypes never materialized. The club's enchanting companions were obliging, honest, and quick to laugh; in fact, they proved far easier to handle than the hell-bent pricks he had tried to please in Manhattan and the Square Mile. B movies and junk novels portrayed working girls as devils or saints, but that was bogus. None of the women of the house could have passed for one of his pious sisters, but there was nothing to fear from them, and more than good looks to admire. Bucky had expected them to do nothing but smoke and drink and screw, but if sex for pay was a part of their lives, it was clearly not the most vital part—daily, the girls proved themselves to be far more than hollow playthings. The tip-off was Natalie's PhD studies, but this was just the start: Kandy spent her off hours crafting exquisite Thai Nang puppets, Linnea taught ballet classes at a girls' school three afternoons each week, and during breaks, Amanda entertained with impromptu recitations of Nora Helmer's best scenes from *A Doll's House*. Every one of the girls had a passion or pursuit outside the club; sex work was simply a means to let them enjoy what they truly loved.

Yet beneath it all was a deeper worry, an essential question he had tried to ignore since his rash decision in the Tottenham pub. What kind of partner would Yuri Pavlovitch Dolgorukov turn out to be? During the hundred-hour weeks of the remodeling, Yuri had labored tirelessly, revealing himself as a style-and-structure mastermind. No one could fault him for the breathtaking manor he had engineered and brought to life. And without prompting, he had regularly offered up more palladium bars, urging, "You will need money for yourself, *tovarish!*" They had never quarreled over the direction of the business, and Yuri had taken time to draw him out about his family, his education, and his years of work for Wall Street, even commiserating with him drunkenly over the shattering breakup with Dayna. Yet Bucky still had doubts. Maybe it just was the New Yorker in him, the part that saw everyone as either a proven liar or a rogue clever enough to cover it up, so far.

There had been *one* surprise: he'd assumed that Yuri would

bring his wife and sons to London at the earliest chance, but his partner had put it off. The explanation was clear enough. Deepening crevices etched the corners of his eyes, bearing out the powers of time and nicotine, but whenever Fabiana was near, Yuri moved and laughed like a boy in love. As proof of his affection, he had draped an emerald necklace across the Brazilian beauty's silken chest, and presented her with a Chanel handbag stuffed with French perfume and fifty-pound notes. And while she refused his invitation to crawl the pubs of Little Russia, she accompanied him daily into the Adventurer's Bedroom. Through the door their feral cries resounded.

Bucky waited until Yuri had his fun a dozen times, then couldn't hold his tongue. "Can't you see she's half your age?"

Yuri rubbed his crotch. "Here, on shaven parts, she has thunderbolt tattoo. In wettest dreams you cannot conceive our passion."

Bucky shook his head in dismay, but Yuri was certain he was in the right. "It is only natural to partake in pleasures of house! You are young man, do you not feel desire?"

If he had been asked the question months earlier, before finding himself in such a favored position, Bucky would have sworn that he would carve a lusty path. It seemed almost an article of faith, the sort of thing you were expected to trot out quickly in any locker room, right after the boasts about a winning season or a personal best on the bench press. But somehow the availability of more than a dozen lovely and skillful partners did not interest him, even now that time had passed since the end of his New York affair. At first he wondered if something was physically wrong; there had never been a "problem" during the years he had lived with Dayna, at least when work hadn't sapped his energy. But the idea of paying for the ladies of the club extinguished any erotic fire. He questioned whether they laughed about him behind his back, or speculated that he wasn't fully a man. That only lessened the attraction.

At the same time he felt a growing attraction to Angelica Smuts. Like any American man, he had always believed that a British accent made a woman more desirable, but Angelica's South African variation sent him tumbling over the falls. Her clipped verbal precision etched every consonant into glass, and she gave each vowel a sensuous caress. Her temperament was a different matter. No man alive could pass her on the street without a second look, but every growl and snarl was pure *Panthera leo.* This clash of manner and appearance beguiled him, and Bucky found himself inventing reasons to speak to her, scheming to draw her into conversation each time he paid her hefty fees or called with her new appointments. She was correct, but no more. Yet each time she uttered some cutting retort the power of her charisma grew. Sometimes—unable to contain his curiosity—he gave in to the temptation to eavesdrop. He had never directly observed any of her "sessions," as she called them, but it fascinated him to see her confront a well-dressed member at the entry to the dungeon, snapping a crop against her open palm as she commanded, "Get in here, slave, you've got a hiding coming!"

Yuri, too, had noticed Angelica's potent menace. The club's first members were Brits, Canadians, Europeans and the Emirates crowd, Japanese and Chinese entrepreneurs, and the odd Aussie or Kiwi, but a small group of Russians had also joined. Soon many of them requested Angelica's cruel attentions. "They call her Little Beria," Yuri said wistfully. "Great Stalin himself would have admired her skills."

In this and other tastes, Yuri had been proven correct about the allure of alternative sex. Krassy and Sassy attracted dozens of devotees with their acrobatic circus stunts and slippery three-way wrestling moves. "We make you pretzel," Sassy would threaten a hapless punter, twisting her hands as if she were wringing out a dishrag. "We smother you with sweating arse," Krassy would warn, flexing her powerful glutes. By now, Bucky had come to understand a basic brothel lesson: the loftier a man's station in life, the greater the chance his secret passion would be dressing in women's undies, learning to bark and obey like a dog, or pissing up the face of a pretty girl. Yuri made a habit of keeping track of which MPs and government ministers had spent time with each of the girls, and which bankers, barristers, knighted physicians, and military officers had played out their private fantasies. Without exception, the bigger the title, the badder the boy.

After watching these elevated perverts parade through the bedrooms, Bucky hoped the oligarch would prove too ripened to trouble the girls. But Nicolai Vasilievitch Klepakov had his own secret obsession. He appeared like clockwork—twice each week—to spend a full and vigorous hour spanking Knotty Natalie.

Apart from the Boss's peculiar habit, Bucky wondered what else had come to light. Despite the comforting name on their door plaque, suspicious eyes were all about, and one could never be certain what misconduct had been revealed, or to whom. Soon after the club opened, they enrolled a paunchy, middle-aged punter with a reddish face and thinning ginger hair; the Minister for Work and Pensions, he claimed. He seemed harmless—passively enjoying Kandy's full-body Thai massages—but as he arrived for his third visit, the badge came out. Speaking now in his capacity as Deputy Commissioner of Police, he informed Bucky that in the future, not only would his gambling tab and his time with Kandy be comped, but a generous sum would find its way into his pocket, unless he and Yuri preferred to discover the lower levels of Scotland Yard.

"This, I will handle," said Yuri. He disappeared into his private office, returning after he had telephoned Klepakov.

Upon hearing of the policeman's demands, the regal oligarch deemed it wise to pay, and to set aside funds against the cost of future baksheesh. In view of this new requirement, Yuri noted, Klepakov would increase his cut from 25 to 33 percent.

It was the first hint of common greed from the Boss, but in view of the circumstances, Bucky wasn't unduly alarmed. It did prompt him to ask about something that had always eluded him. Why had Klepakov left Mother Russia?

Yuri stroked his chin pensively. "Years ago, Nicolai Vasilievitch apprehended the secret to acquiring great wealth. *It is a thousand times easier to steal a ruble than to earn one.* Why break your back, when by clever ploys you can transfer wealth from men who already possess it?"

"But how did that bring him to Britain?"

"You understand London has more billionaires than any other city?"

"That's primer stuff."

Yuri flashed a knowing smile. "Then what better place to hunt rich *suki*?"

■ ■ ■

By now he had mastered the Tube, but getting around underground left Bucky with no means to return with bulky cargo. When vendors couldn't deliver to the club, he used Will Beard's cab as a haulage service, secretly looking forward to the driver's learned discourse. Waiting at the curb for a pickup, he would pretend to check his phone or follow the flow of traffic, then spin around toward the German Embassy, causing a curtain to be drawn in a window high above the street. Pervasive surveillance was new to him, but he had grown more aware of the flocks of video cams perched on London's street lamps and corner ledges. He counted them on walks through the city, tallying dozens, then hundreds of unsleeping lenses. He navigated the city with a strange sense of unease, like a boy who has committed some forbidden act, who lives in fear of being found out.

One drizzling afternoon he summoned Beard for another errand, expecting him to be subdued by the wet weather. Instead he arrived in an energized state. "How I wish you could have been here for my Shakespeare party this past Saturday," he enthused, as Bucky tumbled into the back of the cab. "It was among the most memorable that I have hosted in years. And you would have fitted in perfectly, sir, because contrary to my usual custom, I organized a gentlemen's evening."

"Sorry I couldn't make it."

"I invited the highest and the lowest, as it were. All the kings were there, all the Henrys and Richards, King Lear and King Lewis, King John, King Edward, King Claudius, even Priam and Menelaus, but also all the fools, Touchstone, Feste, Bottom, Pompey—"

"Wasn't Pompey a Roman general?" Bucky interrupted.

"He was, but the Pompey that I invited is a tapster in the employ of Mistress Overdone, in *Measure for Measure*. So Pompey the Pimp and the other fools set out to do what fools do best, which is speak truth to power. After drinks all around, Henry V starts laying it on thick, 'This other Eden, demi-paradise, this fortress built by nature for herself against infection and the hand of war...' but Lear's fool, the brightest of the bunch, puts him in his place. 'When every case in law is right, no squire in debt nor no poor knight; when slanders do not live in tongues, nor cutpurses come not to throngs; when usurers tell their gold i' th' field, and bawds and whores do churches build: then shall the realm of Albion come to great confusion.' Well, I tell you, sir, I thought swords might be drawn! So I stepped forward, insisting, 'Peace, ho! No outrage, peace! The man is noble and his fame folds-in this orb o' the earth.' And luckily, that forestalled an outbreak of violence."

"Sounds like a blowout, but I've been swamped."

Beard seemed concerned. "Is all going to plan, sir?"

"Better than we hoped…we're signing up dozens of new members."

"How marvelous! Her Grace inquired recently as to your progress."

"You can tell her we're crushing it. How is she, anyway?"

"Well and full of plans. I'm driving her to a grand soirée, this coming week. It's a benefit meant to attract the donor class. Her Grace is keen to help a local charity fund a home for wayward girls. There's more than enough of those in Greater London."

"I wouldn't know anything about that," Bucky said, quick to cut off a dangerous line.

When they returned, he declined Beard's offer of help, ferrying his packages into the house in multiple trips. On each return to the curb, he marked how the peeking Teutons observed him from above. For a moment he considered waving to them, thinking it might shame whoever was on over watch duty. But he thought better of it. Suppose they were to stroll over and introduce themselves, even ask for a tour of the club? Better, he thought, to keep his quiet distance, as would any proper Brit.

At month's end the soaring balance of their operating account laid to rest any doubts—their revenues flowed like a spring torrent. Even with Klepakov skimming a fatter share, and the house footing the bill for his smacking fetish, profits grew with every week. They had the girls' share to consider, and wages for the staff; they paid outlandish bills for liquor and food, supplies and services. But a full two-thirds of the balance was theirs to keep. Still Bucky wasn't taking his newfound wealth for granted. After the cons and schemes he had witnessed on the Street, he feared that the cruelest shafting would come when the big boys trashed the major currencies. Untold trillions of debt and mountains of dog-shit derivatives—it could only end with starving schmucks pushing their cash-filled barrows to the grocery. He opened a personal account through the City branch of a Zurich bank, in which his deposits of British pounds were automatically converted into equal portions of Swiss francs and Singapore dollars. With the remainder of his earnings he bought Bitcoins. Feeling secure again—and paying nothing for food or rent—he treated himself to every possible toy, from the latest phones and tablets to a portable hi-rez audio player and a set of esoteric headphones that set him back more than a Savile Row suit. He had never cared about clothing, but he had come to see that his wardrobe marked him as a Yank from twenty paces, something he now wished to avoid. He donated everything he had brought with him from America and then filled his closet with British gear: stovepipe pants and long-toed shoes, a dark woolen pea coat and a dozen T-shirts with the names of bands unknown across the Atlantic. And he threw away his pocket comb and took to tousling up his hair.

As he stood before a mirror, indistinguishable from any West End hipster, he wondered if it was just an outward show or the harbinger of deeper changes yet to come. Before his years in New York he had never understood that a city could transform a man, but slowly, almost imperceptibly, Manhattan had changed him. Maybe it had been the frenetic pace, or the noise and the downtown energy, or maybe the way that time became as valuable as money, so that wasting a moment of anyone's day was tantamount to stealing. After a month he had learned to turn his back on anyone who bored him. After three he had realized that with his friends, he no longer used the phrase, "I have to disagree with you on that point," instead saving valuable seconds with "G'fuckyahself." He couldn't be certain if London would alter him further, or what the changes might be, but it felt as if a transformation was coming.

Yuri seemed unimpressed with Bucky's new clothes and techno-toys—in the wake of the club's roaring success, he had a grander concept of personal reward. He took delivery of a bespoke Bentley convertible in revolutionary red, with leather like a woman's inner thighs and a burr walnut dash and waistrails. The crimson beast was fitted out like a private railway car of the Belle Époque; the rear armrest concealed a bottle cooler and a leaded crystal service, and flush panels on the seat backs folded down into polished picnic tables.

Yuri spent a morning mastering the complex controls and electronics, learning to raise and lower the canvas top and load up the multi-disc changer with his favorite Russian music. Then he installed Fabiana in the passenger seat, promising a London sojourn. In the rear, Bucky lounged at the center with his arms encircling Krassy and Sassy, all of them half drunk and hungry for a top-down ride. They dashed out of Belgrave Square with abandon, snaking through the curves until they came abreast of the Palace, where the circus began. Tourists assumed they could only be royals. The gawkers shouted and leaped, pressing forward with cameras held high, threatening to surround the car until Yuri gunned the monstrous engine and sent them careening down Birdcage Walk, accelerating the length of St. James's Park in a shocking rush of torque. Round Parliament Square they dashed, gaudier than the soaring clock tower and more majestic than the Abbey; they rolled along Victoria Street past the Metro Police and the Ministry of Justice to shouts and photo flashes. Now Yuri threw the car into a broad arc, gathering up Pimlico, Chelsea, and Earls Court into his hands, sweeping along the boulevards of Knightsbridge until the circle rounded and they processed up Cromwell Road. As they motored eastward, the elaborate facade of the Natural History Museum appeared on their left; the sidewalks teemed along the lush lawns to a point beyond the Victoria & Albert, and Yuri slowed the Bentley's pace, inviting adulation.

The throng pulled up to gape, and sensing that they had captured all eyes, Fabiana suddenly pushed upright, statuesque, her arms outstretched like Christ the Redeemer of Rio. Down the length of the block she flung out a cry of joy that spoke for them all: *"Haaiieeeeee!"*

SEVEN

Apart from occasional eruptions of volcanic violence, Jackie Wax existed in a state of benign serenity. Bucky would find him on a stool behind the bar, whistling off-key versions of Morrissey anthems, a half-empty Guinness at his side and a pencil in one of his massive hands to mark up the forms for the dog tracks. If Yuri's passion was discordant Russian music, Jackie's was English greyhounds; any time away from his family—and every penny of his spare cash—was spent at the tracks. He talked devotedly about Romford, Sittingbourne, and his habitual destination, Crayford Stadium, recounting details of races from years past, and stories of champion dogs and their trainers. Their hulking bouncer had an almost clerical cynicism about the nature of men, and absolute faith in the redemptive value of smashing drunken faces. But dogs he viewed with a childlike and all-forgiving love.

"It's no secret you don't have a girl, guv'nor," he announced to Bucky one afternoon. "Leaves a man with no one to talk to. Have you ever thought of getting a dog? There's a program that finds good homes for retired hounds from the tracks. Far better to have the run of this barn than for the poor animal to be cooped up in a flat somewhere."

Bucky was about to ask what kind of dog would be at home in a cathouse. Instead he promised to think it over.

"I could fix you up straightaway," said Wax. "The companionship might do you good."

A week later he advanced his plan for Bucky to better appreciate dogs and domestic life. "I'm off Sunday, and the missus and I would love to have you come by the cottage for tea. Afterwards we can watch the greyhounds run. Some of me pals will be at the Stadium, they're a notorious lot that I'm sure you'll get on with."

Bucky could think of no way to refuse. On Sunday he set out by Tube and train to Kent, hoping to return in time for dinner. He had tried to anticipate just how awkward his visit might be—suppose the fearsome Jackie Wax lorded it over his family? He pictured a cowed wife concealing a black eye under pancake makeup, and disciplined children trembling in fear. Outside the carriage window, southeast London sprawled from Greenwich to Dartford in vast residential tracks that bore no resemblance to the government and tourist districts. After a brief walk from the station, he located Jackie's tidy home on a lane of brick and mock-Tudor dwellings, most with a tree or two shading their well-tended gardens. Roses bloomed in a range of hues, throwing off a pleasant perfume even as he approached the door uneasily. He wondered if it might be possible to call for Wax and avoid being drawn inside, but the pretty, smiling woman who answered his knock all but dragged him into her parlor. He had arrived in the middle of a family discussion, with the two girls, who looked to be about ten and seven, pulling at their father's arms.

"Will you take us to ballet tomorrow, Daddy? Will you watch us practice pliés at the barre?"

"Of course I will, my darlings," Wax said with a look of contented amusement. "I shall give you my full concentration. But now let me speak with Mr. Newman."

Bucky took in the scene. The interior was divided into

smallish rooms, with dark furniture and low ceilings that gave the place the air of a dwelling out of Dickens. This first impression was contradicted only by an inexpensive stereo and console television that hugged the wall opposite the sofa. Over the mantle was a framed studio photograph of Wax, his wife, and the two girls as toddlers; below and to one side stood a wedding photo, and opposite, another picture of Wax at twenty, in military uniform.

Sharp yipping came from the rear of the home. "That's just our Westies," said the wife. "They're banished to the garden for the duration of your visit." She ushered Bucky into a snug little dining room, with a table for six that had been set for tea. Cups and saucers were neatly arranged on lace placemats, with linen napkins and silver teaspoons, and she removed a matching cream-and-sugar set from a china cabinet. Central position in the hutch was reserved for a round plate with fluted edges and an image of the Queen, the decorative dish held upright by a small three-legged stand.

"Will you get the teapot, Jackie?" she said. It was not a request. He moved energetically to bring a steaming vessel from the kitchen, passing it to her with a cloth wrapping the handle. "And the tin of biscuits too." She filled Bucky's cup with boiling water, offering him a bowl filled with varied English and herbal teas in bags.

Bucky thanked her, trying desperately to think of anything to say. "Your girls are beautiful" was his best effort, but he regretted it instantly, realizing that she must know the kind of business Jackie worked in. He feared she might assume his interest was unhealthy.

But she responded sincerely, "That's very kind. Did you grow up with brothers and sisters?"

"Three sisters and three brothers. I was the fifth of seven. This was in Buffalo, in upstate New York."

"I have met my share of Americans, but never anyone from Buffalo. Is it an industrial city?

"It *was*, until the steel works closed. That left beer and football."

"I see," she said, her tone more knowing. "Everyone has their own reasons for ending up here, I suppose."

The two girls had taken places side by side at the table. Bucky expected they would begin to fuss and complain, then slap at each other, spill their tea, or knock over the cream before receiving a reprimand and beginning to cry. He had suffered this ordeal countless times in American homes. But the older daughter confidently lifted the teapot and began to serve her sister. "Here, Sophie, let me fill your cup."

Their mother looked on approvingly. "Well done, Amelia."

"What do you do in London, Mr. Newman?" asked the precocious Amelia. Wax and his wife paled with apprehension.

"There are many gentlemen's clubs in central London for professionals and politicians. I manage one, and your father helps me in the operation of the club."

"You mean like the Reform Club?" she asked, to Bucky's utter amazement.

"That's right, but the Reform Club admits both men and woman as members, while our club accepts only men."

"That's not fair. I should be able to join when I am old enough!"

Wax's wife looked stricken, and Jackie abruptly changed the subject. "Jennie does the books at the Pasha's Palace in Soho, where we met. She's a Yorkshire girl and has a better head for numbers than me." He reached out to gently squeeze her hand.

"Perhaps your family can come over sometime," she said to Bucky. "Have they ever visited England?"

"I'm the first. The rest have never traveled internationally, unless you count the Canadian side of Niagara Falls." The possibility of a family visit had never occurred to him until that moment, and the thought of the explanations he would owe filled him with dread. Hardly a week went by without a breathless note from home—his mother or one of his sisters inquiring, *Are you a knight yet? When will you meet the Queen?* He shuddered and remained silent throughout the rest of their time at table, watching the interplay among Wax, his wife, and their model children.

Finally safe in Jackie's rusting Rover, Bucky thanked him for the hospitality and complimented his house, his garden, his wife, his daughters, his tea service.

"We'll have something stronger as soon as we join up with me mates. I try not to drink around the missus and the girls."

At Crayford Stadium, three men of Wax's age stood by the edge of the parking lot—two hard-faced Brits, one all sinew and bone and the other built like a fireplug, and a lanky black Caribbean with a frizzy tower of hair like a shako. All three were smoking; the tall black man was eating some kind of sandwich from a paper wrapper, alternating bites and puffs. One of the other men held a can of lager; he seemed unsteady on his feet.

Wax eyed him disdainfully. "Carry on like that and you'll be trolleyed before dark."

This drew a laugh and a snarky reply. "You can't drink all day…unless you get started in the morning."

"Here's me boss, Mr. Newman," said Wax, "and these are Privates Atkins and Rolle, and Corporal Hobart."

"You were all in the army?" Bucky asked, trying to be sociable.

Hobart, the brawny corporal, spoke up for the group. "We was with 2 Para in the Gulf, serving under the Colour Sergeant." He motioned toward Wax to acknowledge his former rank. "We was just lads then, but lads you could count on. Still can, if anybody wants to know."

Inside they made directly for the bar, led by the Caribbean Rolle, who seemed impatient for a drink. With full glasses in each hand, they found seats inside the gallery; the second race had started and the dogs flew past in a blur of legs and muzzles, accompanied by shouts of encouragement and disappointed moans from men whose wagers hadn't paid.

"Are you a betting man?" Atkins inquired.

Bucky had never placed a bet on a horse, much less a greyhound. "I wouldn't know which dog to pick."

The gang of four burst into uproarious laughter. "He wouldn't know which dog to pick, did you hear that?" When their amusement had worn off, Atkins said, "All you need to know is who to ask, to be properly tipped. And that would be me."

Bucky was incredulous. "You're saying it's all fixed?"

Another round of wild laughter went up. "What good would it be if it wasn't? You'd likely as not lose all your money!"

Hobart weighed in again. "Don't you worry, Newton, we'll tell you what bets to lay down. In the third race, put your money on the number five dog to place. And in the fourth, play the seven dog to win, and two to show." They all took out their wallets, handing over crumpled bank notes to Atkins, who was apparently the money handler. Rolle and Wax dictated complex bets to win, place, and show across multiple races, as Atkins committed it all to memory with seeming ease.

The fixed races and the bungle with his name annoyed Bucky, and he decided to have it his own way. He picked the favorites for the fourth and fifth races from a track program, and thrust a fresh fifty-pound note toward Atkins, grumbling, "Twenty-five quid on each of them to win."

Wax and his chums let out a collective "Oi—" at this

reckless act, but Atkins palmed the fifty and disappeared for the betting window. He returned minutes later, handing each man a stack of paper betting slips.

Bucky quickly lost his money, while Hobart's precise forecast returned a tidy profit to each of the other men. He sucked his second glass of beer, consoling himself that the wager had been relatively small. The crowd in the glassed-in gallery had swelled—every seat was now taken. During each of the races, the roars and cries were so deafening that Wax and his friends had to bellow into each other's ears to make themselves heard. But Jackie was in his element, downing great gulps of draft as the fleet greyhounds tore past again and again. Bucky had a vision of him in retirement, decades hence, blissfully spending every day at the track. Their brawling bouncer was turning out to be a different sort of man than he had imagined.

In the seventh race the three dog opened a sizable lead, and Rolle edged forward in his seat, fists clenched. When his pick crossed the line a winner he leaped to his feet. "Jah rule! Praise him, *praise* Jah!"

As Rolle ran off to collect his winnings, Wax offered his critique of the day. "Can you think of a better way to spend a Sunday, guv'nor? And how's this for posh company?"

On the train back to central London, Bucky thought about the secret he'd been keeping. He hadn't been ready to admit to Wax that his true hope for companionship wasn't to adopt a dog or host a family tea party, but to draw Angelica Smuts into deeper conversation. Better yet, to persuade the dark-haired domme to join him at the glitzy restaurants, theaters and cultural attractions that London boasted in abundance. He had no intention of visiting her dungeon, but her charisma had cast a powerful spell, and he yearned to engage her one-on-one. In the months since launching International Fulfillment he had been forced to surrender his time to the club. Now, with a stable roster of girls and staff—and any bond with Dayna wiped away—he felt a growing sense of freedom. He read about an art exhibition showcasing works by the finalists for a prestigious prize; after reviewing the article until he could discuss it glibly, he persuaded Angelica to accompany him.

The weather was uncharacteristically dry and warm, and he suggested that they walk to the gallery, which stood on the Embankment, south of Parliament. It was half an hour on foot. He thought it might invite an extended chat. In his own artistic endeavor, earlier that week, he had helped Yuri hang a series of eighteenth-century oils in the Grand Saloon. The portraits of bloated aristocrats and bucolic landscapes were intended to elevate the tone in the bar. He tried it out with Angelica as an icebreaker. "Did you notice those new paintings? They really make an impression."

"The only impression that interests my clients is the one my riding crop makes on their arses. I've never seen two men so house-proud! You should let the maids look after your mansion, and focus on more productive things."

Bucky took it as a chance to draw her out. "What kind of home did you grow up in? You never spoke about it."

"That's because it's none of your business," Angelica snapped. "But if you're curious enough to ask, I suppose I can tell you. I lived on a farm in northern Gauteng, outside Pretoria. I was an only child and was home-schooled, so I had no other children to play with. But I had a pet cheetah that my mother rescued as an abandoned cub, and nursed with milk from a bottle until she could eat solid food. I used to run after her through the fields, though as you can imagine I could never keep up. What a beauty! I never loved another living thing that way."

Bucky tried to picture the scene, then realized it must have been many years earlier. He had no idea of a cheetah's life-span. "Do your parents still have the cat?" he asked.

"A bastard shot her when I was fifteen. I took a different view of men after that."

They were cutting down Eccleston Street across Eaton Square, the rush of buses and hurtling bicyclists posing the usual dire threat. Bucky dodged a motorcycle as he quoted from coverage in the *Times*: "The exhibition presents four artists, but two are especially talented. There's a ceramist who made a series of vases on controversial themes, and a plastics artist who put together something called *The Tree of Corruption*. The critics say they upend every traditional concept of British art. For some reason that reminded me of you."

Angelica glared savagely. "Is that supposed to be an insult?"

"Not at all! What I meant was, you turn traditional concepts of love on their head. Think of yourself as the artist, with a whip instead of a paintbrush."

"Watch yourself. There's only so much I'll put up with, even from a source of income."

At the gallery they entered a series of rooms dedicated to the artists short-listed for the prize. The first salon offered a "floor installation"—a printed guide suggested this phrase—in which great industrial gears, wooden wagon wheels, toilet seats, round serving platters, tractor tires, vinyl record albums, a manhole cover, and half a human skull sliced above the ears had been arranged in crafty patterns. A wall plate named the work *Vicious Circles*. In the next room the floor was bare, but the walls had been hung with fourteen rectangular canvasses, all of the same massive dimensions and all uniformly black. Bucky moved from one canvas to the next, expecting to detect subtle differences in shade, texture, or even brush technique, but they were identical: black, black, black. The dour grouping was titled *False Gods*.

Angelica glowered. "I thought you said these people were high-toned. I could throw pasta against the wall and do better than these piss artists."

"Let's check out the others," Bucky suggested, suddenly feeling ill at ease. In the next room a dozen pedestals had been placed at random; atop the pedestals were glazed vases of varying heights and shapes, in shades of sickly green and blue with blots of crimson. To his disgust, half of the vases had been painted with scenes of a strange man molesting boys and girls. The others presented images of the same wretch in drag and makeup.

Now Angelica was fuming. "Don't ever call *me* a pervert. If I get my claws into the sod who made this shite, I'll tear off some parts he's bound to miss!"

"The last room is the prizewinner," Bucky countered, "maybe it's more uplifting." They entered the final salon, where a fancy blue rosette and ribbon confirmed the judges' blessing. *The Tree of Corruption* stood as if rooted at the center of the room, its broad plastic trunk rising toward the ceiling, crooked branches extending outward. From the plastic branches hung plastic intestines, plastic eyeballs and optic nerves torn from plastic heads, dead plastic cats and rats and rotting plastic garbage, plastic insects and excrement, and even a mutilated human plastic corpse. Bucky took Angelica's arm and steered her from the room, choking, "Why don't we get coffee?"

"Look, Bucky," she said during the uncomfortable return, "if you're going to drag me all over London, let's do something entertaining. There's a club in Brixton called Cruel Britannia. On Saturdays it's amazing after midnight. But you must dress in fetish gear or a mask to get past the doorman."

Exuberant at the invitation, he persuaded Yuri to loan him the Bentley for the following Saturday night. When the evening arrived he brought up the car, honking the horn three times as arranged. A moment passed, then the door of the Belgrave Square house flew open and Angelica marched out, costumed in the black uniform of an SS *Obersturmbannführer.* On her head was a high peaked cap with a leather brim and a silver death's head; a swastika blazed on her red armband. As she descended the steps her jackboots slapped the stone, the light of the street lamps reflected in their gleaming leather.

Bucky glanced toward the German Embassy—the curtains had been opened at a window on an upper floor. A diplomat stared down at Angelica in open-mouthed horror.

"You're being watched!" Bucky called out, pointing toward the observer.

Angelica whirled around and threw out her arm in a Hitler salute, clicking the heels of her boots. Above her, in the embassy, the curtains closed in a rush. She slid into the car and dropped a coiled bullwhip across the armrest, bitching, "You're certainly dressed to the nines. I'll be shocked if they let you in."

Bucky wore black, but it was ordinary street clothing. He intended to make himself presentable by donning a Guy Fawkes mask at the last moment before entering the club. Wary of Angelica's Boer roots, he had never breathed a word to her about politics, but faced with her outrageous attire he couldn't bite his tongue. "You show up dressed as a fascist killer and then criticize *my* clothes?"

Angelica laughed scornfully, "You're so naïve, Bucky, even for an American. Do you think that I'm a *real* Nazi? People love to wear militaria to the clubs. It's part of the fetish scene. You'll see plenty of uniforms tonight, so don't start trembling with fear at the men in Soviet hats and jackets, they're not fire-breathing communists."

On the edgy streets of Brixton he found a spot for the Bentley in front of a late-night liquor store. He hoped the light and the open door would deter the locals from stripping the car to the frame. As Angelica emerged onto the sidewalk he felt a sheepish embarrassment about parading down a London block with a woman in SS uniform, but as they neared the nightclub, he realized that he was the odd man out. Streams of bizarre figures in PVC, leather, or lingerie approached from every direction, lifted high on platforms or skyscraper heels, their features transformed by garish makeup, oversize piercings, and stabbing crested hair spikes. The doorman nodded in recognition as Angelica approached, then scowled at Bucky's black jeans and pullover, raising a hand to block his entry until he donned the mask. Angelica touched the lug's beefy forearm with her whip. "He's with me." A twitch of his head directed them through the door.

A winding staircase beckoned to them from the entryway, turning sharply as it climbed. Bucky followed tentatively as Angelica drew him up the steps, past queens in burning drag and women in bottomless leather chaps; round topless subs jerked to and fro by chains and choker collars. Knots of revelers clustered on the landings, and Angelica raised her whip in greeting as she was recognized. A throbbing electronica beat grew louder at each level. On the third landing a passageway opened onto a curving corridor where a series of doors revealed small stark rooms. As he passed the doorways Bucky glimpsed, in searing flashes, a naked blonde being bound to a trestle, three couples entwined like mating pythons, and a fat man in a gas mask having his shaven genitals flogged by a towering pink latex transvestite.

Nothing he had witnessed at the Belgrave Square house could rival this garden of nasty delights, but Angelica barely noticed, dragging him toward the source of the pumping rhythmic noise. As they entered the dance hall hidden subwoofers massaged their lungs and spleens, and colored strobes exploded as a disco ball scattered fragments of light across the floor. The costumed crowd partied and preened, teetering on their heels or fondling each other in the darkened corners near the bar. On a raised platform at the front of the room, a couple in head-to-toe chains and leathers gyrated with the house track. Behind them a black-and-white video loop flickered on a stained projection screen, serving up hydrogen bomb blasts, surgical gore, and clips of '50s sci-fi monsters reveling in alien rape.

"Luscious!" Angelica cried, her eyes glowing with a fire that Bucky had never seen. She pushed him toward the bar. "Get me a Stellenbosch sauvignon blanc, and don't do anything stupid."

He worked his way to the front of the crowded bar and shouted an order. As he waited for the drinks a young woman in steampunk getup appeared at his right. She placed an electrical device on the bar; the contraption had a thick handle with a blown-glass tube at one end that glowed like a neon sign.

"What the hell is that?"

"Just my violet wand. Want to see how it works?" Without waiting for an answer, she held it an inch from Bucky's right buttock and it fired a crackling bite of current.

"Christ that stings!" The smell of ozone wafted up as he rubbed the pain.

The girl laughed. "That's nothing, luv. You should try it on the tender bits for a proper thrill."

At the opposite end of the disco Angelica had seized control. She strode to the platform and shoved the leather couple into the crowd, capturing the stage. The DJ cued a rapid riff, knowing what was coming. Frenzied men rushed forward in a wave, summoned by the sound; they dropped onto their bellies before the stage, writhing like maddened supplicants.

Angelica cracked her lash above their heads in a string of pistol-shot reports. "Crawl, my little worms," she howled above the din. "Don't make me be harsh with you!"

Bucky threw back his first whisky and called for another as the room began to spin. Many, many rounds later he told Angelica that he'd had enough.

But she refused to leave. "Dressed like that you can take a cab. Leave me the keys, I'll bring Yuri's baby back in the morning." Dulled by fetish and alcohol, he foolishly agreed.

An hour after dawn he awoke to a racket—Yuri was pounding furiously on his door. Outside the house the Bentley had been jammed into a gap at a cockeyed angle. Two of the enormous tires were flattened, deep gouges like fingernail scars disfigured the sleek metal flanks, and the soft leather interior had been defiled by human waste. In a final indignity, the proud "flying B" emblem had been torn from the bonnet and shoved up the car's chrome tailpipe.

"I swear it was fine when I left it with Angelica," Bucky pleaded.

When confronted, she denied a role, hissing, "Drunken yobs from the council flats did it out of spite. Say it was idiot vandalism on your insurance claim."

Jackie Wax had a different perspective. He took Bucky aside, as if he were telling a hard-drinking friend there was nothing for it but to finally get sober. "I'll say it plain, guv'nor. I struggle to picture Miss Smuts in an apron, cooking your Sunday dinner. What about finding an old-fashioned girl who can make a home and give you some children?"

EIGHT

Yuri had always predicted the club's membership roll would swell with hot-blooded big shots and the amoral über-rich. Time had proved him right. Senior MPs and government ministers, securities moguls and manic entrepreneurs, desert princelings, overpaid sportsmen and cunning capital schemers had found their way to the Belgrave Square house. Invariably they asked the same question, *Is it true, what I hear?* Bucky was no stranger to wealth—he had known plenty of men in Manhattan whose savvy stock picks and real estate flips had vaulted them into the penthouse set. But in London he realized that a measly hundred million pounds or euros counted for nothing. In the new century, real wealth was measured in billions.

And Yuri meant to claim his share. Shuffling a deck with liquid ease, he whirled five cards onto a tabletop. "What is this?" he asked in his schoolmaster's voice, as he turned over the cards to reveal a straight flush to a king.

Bucky named the hand, uncertain what Yuri had in mind.

"You must see past mere combinations. This is harpoon for hunting whales."

Like a winter breeding ground, the no-limit card table in the Grand Saloon attracted the leading leviathans. The casual gamblers might while away time at twenty-one before they disappeared with their favorite girl, but the serious players—men for whom poker was the purest form of private enterprise—marched directly to the oval battlefield. For all their cash, the whales preferred to gamble property; the wager of a golden cigarette case or the keys to a Berlinetta was more stimulating to their risk glands than competing for a pile of chips. Late into the night the club's wealthiest won and lost cars and yachts and Mediterranean villas, thoroughbred racehorses and wholly owned subsidiaries. When the stakes were irresistible and the players fully gassed and lubed, Yuri would slide into an open seat and ante up with palladium bars. He had managed to take down a Danish bond dealer for a handsome sailing craft, and an Indonesian oilman for a patch of producing Sumatran wells, but he longed to skewer a real trophy—the club's first bona fide billionaire, Fang Xiaogang.

Fang was an unlikely Croesus, a diminutive karaoke fiend with thick glasses, three smartphones, and seven personal estates. His galaxy of plants and workshops churned out cosmetics, cameras, camping gear, cleaning products, cribs and cars seats, candy and Day-Glo condoms. But that was only the lesser part of the south-China titan's empire. He had bought up half of Dongguan and huge tracks in Shenzhen and Shanghai before speculators chased land prices over the moon. When the market felt toppy, he sold off the less desirable parcels and used the profits to peel away useful Party men from his rivals. Bucky once asked how he had gotten his start, hoping for a tip he could leverage.

"I was rice farmer. Learn all lessons by age of eight."

Each night Yuri stalked and circled his quarry, seeking an opening to lure him into a careless wager. But the mark had a game of his own. Sipping a red lotus cocktail, Fang voiced his admiration for the house, and spun a tale of branded clubs on every continent—Beijing, Bangalore, Berlin, Buenos Aires—all of them as gratifying as the first International Fulfillment location. "I propose exclusive licensing deal," he said grandly. "I will build and operate clubs worldwide, maintaining your high standards. I pay you six percent of net-net profits after taxes, depreciation, and currency conversion, more or less."

"That much?" Yuri scoffed. "What words can express full depth of my gratitude?"

Fang's eyes became slits. "Alternative is wave of knock-off clubs, like Guangzhou Gucci bags. Let us be honest, from this you will make nothing."

"Indeed, let us be honest, since thieves are not."

"You would enjoy many fruitful rewards from such expansion, and gain much face. Consider prudently my generous offer."

When the last member staggered away broke from the tables, Bucky asked if Yuri intended to present the plan to the oligarch. His face twisted into a grimace, as if he'd been offered the chance to pound a nail into his knee. "Six percent of nothing! I have better deal. In exchange for franchise rights, Fang must give his cock to angry goose for special blowjob." He stomped from the Grand Saloon growling profanities.

Yuri's whale hunt was soon interrupted by the only thing that could make him forget about Fang—Fabiana had accepted him as her principal lover. For weeks he had courted and flattered and pursued the Latin beauty, offering up more lavish gifts and rubber-banded rolls of cash. He escorted his quarry to the shops of Knightsbridge, and chauffeured her on weekend getaways throughout the south of England, until the ravaged Bentley was hauled away.

His strategy had worked, but the price of love was steep: Fabiana wanted to make him over as a younger man. First, Yuri's tired borscht-and-blini diet came in for improvement. At trendy Brazilian bistros, she introduced him to vatapá, feijoada, and cururu de camarao. Course by course, she sought to persuade him that wildly different spices could somehow coexist in food—onion mixed with mint leaves, garlic on top of red chili pepper—and Yuri's vodka stock vanished, replaced by an array of exotic cocktails. But beyond even food and drink, Fabiana's greatest love was dance. At a club near Drury Lane she began teaching Yuri the maculelê and the challenging lambada zouk. Her partner tried to copy her lithe gyrations, but he appeared to be a lost explorer set upon by driver ants, desperately trying to stamp his attackers into the floor of the Amazon jungle. When he realized that the laughter in the club was at his expense, he drowned his embarrassment with a caipirinha. More skillful partners took his place, showing off their youthful moves. When one of the agile boys launched into a flurry of leaps and turns, Fabiana cried out in delight, clapping her hands.

From Yuri's struggles, she concluded that he needed to become more elastic. She enrolled him in a yoga class, conducted in a room as blazing as a foundry, and dragged him to a health club with an Olympic pool, where she set him to a regimen of lap swimming until he swallowed water and all but drowned. When he refused to embark on any more hazardous deep-end voyages, they compromised on jogging around the Serpentine in the park. But for all these determined steps—and in spite of their passionate connection in bed—they faced an intractable problem. To Fabiana, Yuri's Slavic turn at English was barely lucid, while her woolly pronunciations of Anglo-Saxon words left him baffled. She decided the answer was to teach him Portuguese. She bought him a computer-based language course and a book of common expressions, sternly instructing him, "You learn all of this, *amor!*" But practicing useful phrases such as, "*Você é a mulher mais bonita do mundo, Fabiana,*" caused Yuri to nearly swallow his tongue, and something like underwater Urdu drooled from his weary mouth.

Not that he gave any thought to surrender. Covertly he had undertaken a series of appointments at a Harley Street clinic, which promised to erase a decade from any sagging face. From his room came the grunts and moans of morning sit-ups, and his half-gallon container of sour cream disappeared from the house refrigerator.

Finally Bucky had to say it. "Have you forgotten that you're a married man?"

"What is this to people in love? We will run on the beaches of São Paulo. We will live on coconuts and mangoes! And I forget to ask, do you think she will adore me greatly if I have teeth fixed like film star?"

Days later a letter arrived from Yuri's wife. Someone had tipped her off to the success of the club, and told her the tale of the Bentley. She put together the rest on her own.

"Why do you not write more often, my husband? When will you fulfill your promises? Your bourgeois tastes betray you, and I sense that your heart has been stolen away."

Yuri did not answer; he was obsessed with his own scheme—transforming Fabiana from an escort into an entrepreneur. In his view there was very little difference, apart from prostitutes being prettier, and he reasoned that once his long-legged favorite had a business of her own, she would have no reason to lie down with other men. Fabiana had always adored flamboyant clothing, almost as much as dance. "You will be designer of nightclub wear," Yuri proposed. "You will teach the High Street what it means to dress in sexiest style!"

To his delight Fabiana embraced the idea. Her first creative inspiration was to name her new line "Klub Kloze," and to sketch out a simple logo with two *K*'s, the second flipped around against the first to form an inner diamond. Then she addressed the matter of personnel. She announced that her elder sister Luiza was a seamstress of rare talent and vast experience, and her younger brother Eduardo could handle the books and accounts, if given proper training. "He is very bright, and can help me grow the business," she cooed, stroking Yuri's neck. "Of course he must attend university first."

It was just a sequence of easy steps, in her view—whisk her brother and sister to Britain, enroll Eduardo at an upmarket college, lease a workshop for Luisa stocked with sewing machines and bolts of cloth and a thousand buttons and bangles, hire a gifted designer and some hungry salesmen, then buy up four-color advertising in modish magazines. Yuri swallowed it down with more difficulty than he had the spicy food, but Fabiana's charms won him over. He promised that all obstacles would vanish, and all costs be amply covered.

"What about your own family?" Bucky asked, when he learned of the plan.

"These are different matters, each to be accomplished on its own schedule."

Bucky abandoned the dispute; he had other worries that couldn't wait. He had hired four new girls—one to replace Linnea, who had announced her return to the Norwegian ballet, and three more to handle the ever-rising appetites of members—and each had queries or suspicions, trivial requests or time-consuming favors to ask. With the passage of time, the day-to-day operation of the club had become routine; he had to fight off an impulse to write out a FAQ for new hires and hand it to them when they started. But he feared that if he took this shortcut, his own lack of passion would translate to the same ennui in the bedrooms.

Weeks later, when Luiza and Eduardo passed through Heathrow, visas in hand, Fabiana greeted them with tears and shrieks of joy. She had complained of their long separation, so the touching reunion was much as Yuri had expected. He sat in awkward silence on the train to central London, as the three siblings chattered away in light-speed Portuguese. The language barrier rendered him mute, but worse, Luiza and Eduardo seemed to have no idea who he was, and stranger still, Fabiana had become a different woman. She wore no makeup for the happy occasion, and her luxuriant hair was pulled up under a cap; her faded jeans and plain cloth jacket gave no hint of her usual glamour. Even the emerald necklace that Yuri had given her had been replaced by a simple gold cross on a chain.

"No man can expect the constant love of any woman," he mused to Bucky, recounting the day's events.

"And apparently no wife can expect the constant love of any husband."

Yuri shrugged off the slap, and took up the challenge of coaxing Klub Kloze into the air. Bucky saw little of his partner in the weeks that followed, as Yuri, Fabiana, and Luiza chased their fashion dream. They rented an unheated loft in Southwark and filled it with the machines and materials Luiza required. Next a shiny trade van appeared outside the club, its sliding door freshly painted with the double-*K* Klub Kloze logo. At dawn and midnight, Yuri came and went with a cell phone screwed to his ear, babbling about bolero jackets, peekaboo tops and spaghetti straps, or the mood swings of their latest doe-eyed designer. Finally surfacing, he announced that his birthday would be celebrated at month's end, in a private party attended by all the girls of the house and a troop of his Tottenham friends. To please Fabiana and her sister, he had arranged for a *música popular brasileira* group to play in the Grand Saloon.

Behind the carnival atmosphere was a surprising personal milestone. From the night they first met, Bucky had assumed that his Russian partner was still in his thirties. But on the evening of the party, Yuri revealed that he had reached the age of forty-five. "Nearly half of life complete!" he exulted, one arm gathering Fabiana's waist.

"I read that the average life-span for Russian men is only fifty-eight."

Yuri refused to be wounded. "Here in London, such petty formulas do not apply." He moved away, twirling Fabiana into a samba, aping her delicious undulations. He had spilled a drink down the front of his pant leg, making it appear that he had pissed himself, and one of the tails of his body-hugging shirt came out as he danced, exposing a thin band of white underpants above his jeans. Yet his eyes glistened with youth and gusto, as if he had swallowed some elixir that rolled back the years. He circulated among his friends, laughing and pushing drinks on anyone with an empty glass. The Little Russia crowd was seeing the house for the first time; they licked their lips, wide-eyed, as Ruta, Charlotte, Mandy, and Kandy circulated with trays of meats and sweets. To Bucky's relief, the private bash pulled up short of a brawl—when a reveler slipped a hand under Ruta's knickers and shoved her toward the bedrooms, a terrifying glare from Jackie Wax sent him slinking back to the bar.

Midway through the evening Yuri and Fabiana disappeared; noticing their absence, Bucky assumed they couldn't wait for another roll. But a second surprise was building. The Brazilian musicians were abruptly silent, the overhead speakers began to thump out a catwalk beat, and someone dimmed the lights in the Saloon. From a corridor by the baths Fabiana appeared in a whirl of fur and fabric, her endless legs and breathtaking bootie enclosed by leopard Capri pants. Above her bare midriff, the taut décolletage had been stuffed into a sequined halter. She strode out bravely on suicide heels, scarlet soles edged with rows of shining metal studs. Her head held up a fascinator of iridescent foil and a blast of bird-of-paradise feathers. As she passed, Bucky realized that her leopard pants were not a print, but sewn from actual skins—Luiza had held back nothing for the show.

"You like?" Fabiana called to the room. "I give you Klub Kloze style!" Wild cheers and whistles seemed to validate her taste, and her sister's bravura needle skills.

"My darlings, you are too kind! But more handsome is Yuri's outfit." She turned and gestured, and from the corridor Yuri made a lugubrious entry, whether from drunkenness or shame, Bucky could not be certain. Fabiana had decked him out in creamy sailor's pants and a pair of tricolor boat shoes, with a rawhide vest and a rakish black gaucho's hat, secured with a little lanyard. Yuri's hairy torso rose and fell beneath the vest, but a more startling accent bulged between his legs. Inspired, perhaps, by the collection in the Entry Hall, Luiza had sewn a leather codpiece into the crotch of Yuri's bell-bottoms.

"Our new masculine style," Fabiana exclaimed. "Look for it in the hottest discos!"

The following morning, as the maids swept up the party mess, Yuri confronted the first day of his downward half. "Is difficult age for any man…certain pleasures begin to slip away. But Fabiana makes me feel like rampant cavalry mount."

Bucky ignored the bedroom boast, he had already heard too many. And he was worried about the clothing line. The eclectic costumes from the previous evening had shown a certain effort at pre-production work, but he had expected that by now, Fabiana would have quit the house for her atelier. Instead, she was still turning tricks for her regulars, while Luiza labored over a sewing machine. And Eduardo hadn't been seen in London since packing off to Manchester to study business accounting.

"Is Klub Kloze making headway? Have they booked any wholesale orders?"

Yuri grinned broadly. "Have no hurry. Revenue will flow when spring collection is released."

"Spring is months away! How much capital will they burn through by then?"

"Is only money, *tovarish*. Remember this when you are my age."

For his partner's sake, Bucky hoped that Fabiana would re-focus her energy on the start-up. But the following month she announced that she would travel to Majorca with Luiza, for a week of sun and a brief escape from the burdens of their fashion empire. Yuri begged to accompany her, to pay every expense, but she insisted that the trip was her only chance for private time with her sister. Days passed without word as Yuri paced and drank. His messages to Fabiana's mobile phone went unanswered, and more ominously, when he called the desk at her hotel, he was told that she had checked out. Then, one afternoon, shortly after letters were delivered, Bucky heard wailing from the kitchen.

Fabiana had sent a postcard. "Yuri darling, I will not return. DJ Fernando is my perfect lover, I will dance to his mix forever. Luiza can run Klub Kloze. Remember to pay her salary."

Yuri laid his head on the table and sobbed, "All is lost!" At his side, Bucky saw a torn envelope and an invoice on university letterhead: the past-due bill for Eduardo's tuition.

▪ ▪ ▪

For all the turmoil of the season, Yuri finally experienced an interval of joy. His beloved Bentley had been repaired—at ruinous cost to his insurance company—and once again it graced a spot before the house, a harbinger of the pleasures that awaited inside the club. He seemed hesitant to drive the sleek convertible, as if he feared new damage. From the window he gazed out at his prize until the light began to fade, musing, "Better than new. A thing of loveliness once more." For weeks Bucky had endured his partner's absent-minded ramblings, as Yuri's inner eye remained fixed on the image of a lissome dancer. Now he hoped that the Bentley's return would nudge him back to life, but every sensuous line only called to mind a greater beauty.

That evening at the poker table Yuri's good fortune returned. Laughing and bantering with the regulars, he voyaged over vodka seas and threw down hand after winning hand; he won a pot of six thousand pounds on a bluff, then beat a Tory MP out of the contents of his wine cellar with three timely jacks. Just after midnight, as if the gods of luck intended an even greater reward, Fang Xiaogang took a seat at the table. Uncharacteristically, his play seemed erratic, even slipshod. He folded what would have been winning hands, and his stake grew smaller through the early hours.

Any player familiar with Fang's shrewd ways might have suspected a ruse, but ripping drunk and up by thousands, Yuri steamed ahead. When Fang exhausted the last of his stake to match a raise, Yuri's manners deserted him.

"Confucius say, man with cards up his arse soon lose bollocks." He took another belt, then shoved a stack of palladium bars toward the pot. "I raise fifty thousand pounds."

Fang dug into his pocket for a set of keys and tossed them onto the bullion. "Maybach 62, a most reliable conveyance. You must put up vehicle of equal worth if you wish to call."

Yuri slapped down the keys to his Bentley and fanned out a full house, aces over queens. He made an insolent grab for both sets of keys, but Fang blocked him—slowly, with patient cruelty, the China Whale turned over four deuces.

"I never drive open convertible. Perhaps now I take my lover for an unforgettable ride." He palmed the keys and left the table, motioning to one of the croupiers to power up the karaoke machine. As the music surged, he began to croon, like a squat, eccentric Elvis, "Wise mahn say, only fool rush in—"

NINE

Soon after these reversals, Bucky suffered a shock of his own. Dayna had been silent since offering her chilly prescription for UK marketing, but now she hurled a bomb in e-mail—she had hooked up with a skyrocket hedge fund manager from Connecticut. *Reggie just made VP and got a whopping bonus. He's asked me to help him design a dream house! And he's taking me to London & Paris. The least we can do is treat you to un bon déjeuner.*

The longer he was apart from Dayna, the more her thinking defied decryption. She expected him to sit at the table like a happy sap with the man who had replaced him, and made it sound as if picking up the tab would square things. But refusing her invitation seemed spiteful and pathetic. And he was curious to see what the new guy offered that he could not, apart from status, wealth, and proximity. Reflexively, he checked the rising balance of his Swiss account—at least the monetary gap between himself and the interloper was growing smaller.

Dayna phoned from the Savoy on the morning they arrived. She raved about the suite and the Thames river view, and informed him that Reggie wanted Mexican food for lunch.

"But this is England! Indian or Italian will be better."

"You're always so critical, even when other people are paying. I already picked a place in Leicester Square. Meet us there in half an hour."

At the table, she inclined a cheek for Bucky's perfunctory kiss, then gave his British clothes and shoes a wide-eyed once-over. "*Très pimpant!*" she said grudgingly. She looked a few pounds heavier, and the slightest bit older than he remembered. Her face was still puffy from the flight, but the greater shock was to see her with another man. He might be over the devastation, but he found out fast that he could still feel jealousy.

Reggie, a tall balding man, maybe thirty-nine, with a slight bulge at the stomach, greeted him warmly as if the matter of Dayna swapping bunks was just business…no different than re-positioning capital assets out of tech and into financials. "Helluva city!" he gushed. "This is what I call living large. *Arriba!*" He swilled most of a margarita, then caught the eye of a waitress and signaled for a refill. "I thought I'd be trashed after that red-eye, but I feel OK. How about you, sweetie?" He rubbed Dayna's shoulders.

"Waking up. At least it's faster getting in from the airport than New York."

"You took the Heathrow Express?" Bucky asked.

Reggie answered for both of them, "We did. Funky train station at the end of the line. It's no Grand Central."

"Paddington Station became the terminus of the Great Western Railway in 1838, so it's not the newest station in London. But it was entirely redesigned by Isambard Kingdom Brunel in 1854—you know Brunel, he's the same man who built the Clifton Suspension Bridge over the Avon Gorge, and the first propeller-driven transatlantic liner."

Dayna stared in astonishment, and Reggie said, "Whoa, *amigo*, how do you know all that?"

"It's just something that any Londoner would be aware of."

Dayna and her new beau had their phones out, angled beside their plates; the gadgets chirped and burped and farted, prompting flurries of stabbing thrusts at the screens. Dayna kept up a side conversation with Reggie about the texts and e-mails that she was receiving, as if she were still at her desk. "I'm sending you the Fentons' slide deck about Paris, the one with the list of furniture stores." He mumbled something in return, staring down at his own screen, clicking rapidly through a list of messages. Bucky had more to say—about Brunel, the financial markets of the City, the heated Parliamentary politics, or anything else about Britain that might interest them—but he was reluctant to disturb their electronic intercourse.

The waitress returned with Reggie's second margarita and a basket of stale tortilla chips that crumbled when scooping the insipid salsa. Dayna didn't care about the lousy chips. "I have amazing news, I've been promoted to Senior Principal Marketing Administrator for Branding. But it gets even better, I've been picked to head up a team of three. We're going to choose the new corporate font and a suite of document templates."

"Thrilling. Will you get a raise?"

She frowned. "That will be performance-based, but it's really not the point. This is a big move up for me, I would have thought you could at least be happy. Anyway, there's more—our new house is to die for. We found a *merveilleuse* subdivision off the Merritt Parkway where everything's 9,900 square feet and up. The builder told us that all our neighbors are investment bankers or have taken start-ups public. Did I mention that Reggie has his MBA in M&A?"

"That's impressive," Bucky said, wishing he could spit a cardboard tortilla chip into his napkin. "Congratulations to you both."

"The kitchen is the best part. We're going to have cherry cabinets and a cerulean blue French stove with six high-capacity gas burners."

"But you don't even cook."

"*Cela prend trop de temps!*" Dayna snapped, flinging up her hand in an almost Parisian display of pique. Bucky needed no translation.

Reggie gulped his drink, then interrupted. "So here's the part that gives me the hots. We paid the local home theater guy to walk the frame and draw up a plan. Picture eleven channels of surround sound and a plasma screen like a Jumbotron. I'm talking Blu-ray out the ass!"

"Almost makes me want to go home."

The food arrived and conversation stalled as Reggie and Dayna began to graze. Bucky had ordered cheese enchiladas, figuring that anything so simple would be invulnerable to a culinary screw-up. He'd been dead wrong—the traditional recipe had been altered to employ an English cheese with a moldy taste and an odor like foul gym socks. Beans and rice squatted on the platter, a congealed lump that defied his fork.

"This is kinda hokey," Reggie grumbled, tucking into the smoking mess on his plate. "People say the food over here is slop, but fajitas aren't that hard to make."

"Try some chicken curry next time. You won't be disappointed."

"You have to show us where you work," Dayna insisted as the check arrived. "Is it far?"

Bucky had anticipated this request, and decided that if he refused, it would arouse more suspicion than a discreet drive-by with some ambiguous blather about "professional services" and "global clientele."

"It's ten minutes away on the Tube, just south of the Palace. Do you have Oyster cards?"

Dayna and Reggie stared at him in mystification.

"We'll take a cab. We can drive past the business and I'll get out at that point. You can keep the cab. I'm sorry the office has a strict policy of no distractions, so I can't invite you in."

"*No problemo,*" Reggie said. "I hear these Brits are pretty goddamn formal."

When the taxi reached Belgrave Square, Bucky told the driver to make the full circle before pulling up in front of the house. "This is the most exclusive neighborhood in London. Most of the units are five floors, in addition to the underground levels. We were lucky enough to acquire the property next to the German embassy." Lunch may have been a plateful of scat, but it was delicious to one-up Dayna's bragging about her elephantine barn.

"What a lovely square," she replied. "Why don't we let the cab go, and walk for a bit?"

Bucky could think of no way to object; as Reggie paid the driver, he glanced anxiously toward the house, wary that someone or something shocking would be coming or going. To his relief all was calm. Only a young East Indian woman stood alone on the sidewalk, between the embassy and the house.

"This way," he said, motioning to Dayna and Reggie.

As they approached the steps, where he intended to say good-bye, the Indian woman appeared to be sizing him up, her eyes shifting down and back from a sheet of paper that she held in her hand. Then she marched directly toward him with a resolute gait, pulling up to block his path. She was slightly built, about his age, with a flawless complexion and piercing eyes.

"Buckminster C. Newman, of International Fulfillment? I demand to speak to you."

Bucky felt a quiver of unreality. "How do you know my name?"

"I looked up the International Fulfillment web domain on Whois. The registrar is Buckminster C. Newman. And I found this picture of you on a social networking site. I recognize you! Are you going to deny it?"

"No, I don't deny it. Who the hell are you?" To one side, Dayna was already clutching Reggie's arm, as if she were ready to flee.

"I am Sangita Sharma, with Devi Way. We help women escape the slavery to which you condemn them."

"Bucky, what's going on here?" Now Dayna was openly alarmed.

Sharma turned to her. "Do you know this man is a whore-monger and an enemy of all women? Do you understand the evil done by him, and other predators like him?"

Bucky took a threatening step forward. "Bullshit! Our girls earn more than an NHS doctor. They work for us because they want to, there's no force."

"How dare you call them girls? You use that only to marginalize them, when they are making you rich. You should refer to them as women if you intend to live off their backs."

"Call them whatever you want, I don't give a damn. But you have no business saying that we're hurting anyone. We offer the best, and the proof is we turn away twenty applicants a week."

"That explains everything," Sharma sneered. "Why didn't you tell us what you're peddling is the finest cunts in Christendom?"

"This has nothing to do with Christianity."

"That is the first honest thing you have said."

The color had drained from Dayna's face, but Reggie seemed energized. He leaned toward Bucky's ear. "I don't know what you're up to, bro, but if I were you, I'd get a sharp criminal lawyer." He spun Dayna around and moved away rapidly, barking, "Don't look back!" when she turned her head.

Bucky couldn't decide whether to curse the little Indian woman or knock her down. In the whole of his life no one had accused him of being a straight-up scoundrel. "Get out of here and don't ever come back," he raged. But Sharma handed him the paper she had been holding, a printout of the profile page with his smiling head shot, from a business networking website that touted his qualifications and contacts.

"What a shame! Shame on *you*, Buckminster C. Newman, for squandering your education and gifts." Then she walked away.

The following two days passed without incident, but Bucky lay awake each night, wondering how much damage the mad zealot could inflict. Would she contact people he knew in New York and try to discredit him? He had no fear of a criminal complaint; they had done nothing directly to injure Sharma, and Scotland Yard was securely bought. But having some jumped-up charity on their tail meant disruption and danger lay ahead. He pondered whether to tell Yuri, but decided to hold back. Sharma had tracked him down—not his partner— and she had made no direct threat against the club.

On the third day, as he began to hope that the episode had passed, Sangita Sharma returned. At midafternoon, with gentlemen abed upstairs and a half dozen of the girls drinking and laughing in the Grand Saloon, angry knocking sounded against the door. Charlotte moved to answer, but Bucky waved her off; he peered one-eyed through the viewport and saw his determined pursuer.

"Go away, you have no business here!" His angry voice drew the attention of everyone in the Saloon, including Jackie Wax, who came out from behind the bar and started down the staircase. To Bucky's dismay, Sharma didn't leave—instead she thrust a rolled umbrella through the mail slot, jamming open the brass flap and nearly skewering his leg. Then she dropped to her knees on the step and began to shout through the opening.

"You women in there, do you realize what will become of you? You are digging your own graves! The men who put you up to this are no better than robbers and murderers."

Bucky pulled out his wallet and drew out all the bills, then pushed the cash through the mail slot. "Just take it and leave."

Sharma shoved back the bank notes, scattering them onto the floor. "You cannot bribe me. Our supporters include two life peers and the Duchess of Saltaire."

Wax had come up alongside. "Just say the word, guv'nor."

"I'll deal with this myself."

Still Sharma cried out through the mail slot. "Do you think of yourself as a decent man? You might as well be Vlad the Impaler! And we know who is backing you, that poisonous toad Nick Klepakov."

A knot of members had come to the balustrade at the sound of a commotion, and now some of the girls descended from the Saloon. Mandy shouted through the door, "Can't you see we're trying to earn a living here? No one gives a flip what you think."

Charlotte taunted, "Why don't you find a boyfriend and tell him to shag you until you come to your senses?" The other girls shrieked with laughter, but outside, Sharma continued to call to them, imploring them to quit the house, to contact Devi Way for escape to a better life.

At last Angelica strode into the entry hall with a dressage whip, her face a furious mask. Through the door she threatened, "Leave now or I'll pull you inside and teach you some manners."

Immediately all was silent. After a short time, hearing nothing and seeing no one through the viewport, Bucky cautiously opened the door. The step was deserted, but from the bushy square, a photographer aimed a telephoto lens at the house. His motor drive whirred.

Bucky secured the door and turned to Wax, Angelica, and the other girls, and Yuri, who had silently appeared. "This is nothing. She's just some freaked-out lunatic."

"Let us discuss the matter privately," Yuri said without cheer.

TEN

Bucky knew it wouldn't end with an umbrella thrust through the mail slot—the only question was how Sangita Sharma would come at them next. The day after the shouting match at the door, an odd assortment of threadbare men and frumpy women appeared on the sidewalk, cradling sheaves of paper. As the girls arrived for their shifts, the Devi Way proselytizers tried to press their leaflets on them. Most declined, but Krassy and Sassy accepted, handing the sheet to Bucky once inside the door.

"A Way of Life or a Way of Death?" said the bold headline. At the left margin was an image of a Bengali girl lying dead outside a brothel. At the right—to Bucky's horror—was his own bright-eyed head shot from the networking page, with the caption "Your heartless victimizer." The rest looked to be boilerplate. "Around the world, sexual slavery and prostitution destroy lives, families, and communities, while ruthless men profit from exploitation and abuse. Visit our website to learn how to combat this curse."

He went directly into his office and brought up the Devi Way site. The home page was amateur hour, he told himself disdainfully, but it served up a riveting photo animation and a lengthy list of criminal abuses. In Birmingham, troops of underage girls were groomed to work as prostitutes. Immigrants had been confined to a filthy cellar in Manchester and compelled to trade sex for food and drink. And Edinburgh had become a northern paradise for enterprising street pimps. Near the bottom of the sinners list was International Fulfillment, with a brief description: "An opulent house of ill repute for well-heeled men of high repute." No members were named or pictured, but the blurb warned, "Our volunteers shall continue their attempts to shutter this nexus of corruption." Far worse, for the first time the club's address had been published.

He read on. Some of the outrages—the website claimed—were opposed by Devi Way through direct action; in more distant parts of Britain, police had been informed and assisted. The charity also operated a women's shelter at Ilford, on the eastern side of Greater London, and offered counseling and substance abuse programs. Under a tab titled "Make a Difference," he found a form for online contributions. "I'm shocked, *shocked*!" he said bitterly to no one, then returned to the leaflet, read it again and tore it into pieces, taking care that his photo was divided and quartered. Of all the blows that Sharma had delivered, the most astounding was how she had uncovered his identity. As obvious as it now appeared, it had never occurred to him that anyone might look up the domain registrar of the club website, then search for a photo and bio corresponding to that name. Following the same process, he confirmed that Sharma was the registrar of the Devi Way site, then found a social page with details on her background. She had read history and literature at the University of East London, and logged three years with the City of London as a family case worker before starting her charity. Her page included hundreds of contacts and sincere recommendations. He searched the property records for Ilford, but came up with nothing matching her name—he concluded that the Devi Way offices and women's shelter were probably rented space. Sharma and her charity seemed to be little more than poorly capitalized street protesters, but the same could be said of movements that had brought down kings and empires. And International Fulfillment wouldn't be that tough a target.

He pushed back from his desk, trying to take it all in. Within the walls of the Belgrave Square house he felt physically secure, but he knew that he had blundered deeply into trouble. Through high school the thumb of the Church had pressed down hard on every neck, and "crime" amounted to adolescent pranks or pilfering some father's liquor cabinet. Even with the paid cheating and petty drug dealing in college, he had never been the one who was caught. Now he was living the nightmare of being naked in a crowd, exposed and scorned, and a sickening wave of fear crashed over him—suppose his family learned what he had done? He imagined his face and film of the house gleefully served up coast to coast as salacious cable claptrap. *An American Whorehouse in London*, they'd call it, or *Bucky, Pimp of Belgravia*. He bolted for the toilet and retched.

Two days later the warfare worsened. On Saturday morning, picketers began to tramp in dogged circles before the club. The marchers were silent and made no move toward the front door, but as Bucky watched, two club members—regular punters of Kimiko and Charlotte—approached the house, pulled up short when they saw the accusatory signs, then turned up their collars and slipped away. He hoped the Devi Way gang would stray onto the property of the German Embassy and be sent roughly packing, but they remained within a tight range until well after dark. Not a single member had entered the club.

Jackie Wax tried to console him. "Pay no mind to that lot. They couldn't organize a piss-up in a brewery."

But Yuri was already thinking ahead. "Tell Laira to call Sunday punters and advise to enter house through alley. And let us imagine all things short of murder to solve this problem."

The following morning the protesters returned to ruin another day. Bucky could think of no way to end the impasse, but at the first of the week he received an unexpected call from Will Beard. He wanted to meet that evening at an ancient pub he frequented on Fleet Street.

"I am aware that certain difficulties have arisen," Beard said with his customary tact, once they were seated in a wooden booth with sweating pints before them. "That is most unfortunate, in view of the success you have enjoyed since coming to London."

Bucky couldn't be certain how much he knew, but Sangita Sharma's claim to have the financial support of the Duchess of Saltaire probably meant that International Fulfillment had been unmasked. He tried to put a brave face on it. "I've seen protests in New York that make those people look like Christmas carolers. I'm not intimidated by jerks in the street."

Beard sipped his bitter. "Certainly not. But you may have friends you're unaware of. I happened to speak with Her Grace yesterday, and she expressed the opinion that if you would negotiate in good faith—"

"Why would she give a damn either way?"

Beard did not respond at once; instead he appeared to be weighing his words carefully before speaking. "When I was a young man, a girl got into the back of my cab one winter night in Pimlico. A lovely girl, big soulful eyes but red from crying. Some drunken prick had knocked her about. I've seen every kind of trouble in my rear-view mirror, and most of it leaves me cold, but that girl had a quality about her—a touching sort of vulnerability—that made me want to wrap my arms around her and protect her. I knew she was a tart, but somehow it didn't matter. We started seeing each other, and let's just say that she was *very* kind to me. You know how people scoff at fools who fall for prostitutes, but it's easier to love one than you might think. Even when she married up into better society, I went on loving her."

With this last part, Bucky got the point of the story. He struggled to maintain his flat expression as the truth about the Duchess sunk in.

Beard went on. "The ninth Duke was much older than her; eventually he passed, and I saw the chance for us to be together again—and to go on looking after her. Her Grace might seem to require no protection, now that she has the Duke's money and the estate, but there's more than a few hard hearts in this country that would love to send her back to the streets. So now you know why I care for her, and intend to watch over her. And you can also understand why she's determined to support Ms. Sharma's charitable work."

Bucky nodded quietly.

"At any rate, she asked me to convey this thought, that in matters of a delicate nature, a gentleman will always choose private conciliation over public acrimony."

Bucky finally answered. "Conciliation is fine, unless the other side wants unconditional surrender and a war crimes trial."

Beard took another drink, savoring a long swallow. "I believe you will find your critics to be more obliging than that. And remember, 'a peace is of the nature of a conquest; for then both parties nobly are subdued, and neither party loser.'"

Bucky was silent again—he was struggling to untangle Beard's words from Shakespeare's.

But the cabbie wasn't through. "In my own experience, the world is not a series of inflexible dualities. You must reach an accommodation—a marriage of sorts—between your own way of life and the lives of others. The most difficult thing for men and nations is to join with their opposites, but in the end it is the one thing that saves them. It might even save you, my young friend."

Bucky finished his drink and told Beard he would consider talking instead of fighting. But when he returned to the house, matters had already taken a more ominous turn. He found Yuri pacing in the Entry Hall, his face dark with worry. Sangita Sharma had contacted Klepakov to warn that Devi Way had photographs of him, and other public men, entering the club. She threatened to publish the images unless the Belgravia house was promptly shuttered. The oligarch had made it clear to Yuri that Sharma's silence would either be bought, or obtained by other means.

"You don't mean his hoodlums are going to start cracking heads?"

"No heads will be broken if there are brains within them. But Nicolai Vasilievitch will deal swiftly with any distractions, so they do not impede his larger plans."

Bucky had always sensed there was more to the oligarch than Yuri had revealed. Now it raised the question, "What's Klepakov really up to? He's not here to build palaces and defraud rich *suki*. Something bigger is going on."

"Certainly, *tovarish*! Our exalted patron has full awareness of his special role in history. He has revealed to me how the life of Britain moves in cycles of one thousand years, each cycle driven by a valiant genius from abroad. In 43 AD, Aulus Plautius conquers savage Britannia. In 1066, William of Normandy subdues King Harold's puny forces. Now our splendid Boss will fulfill the promise of a new millennium. Is it not thrilling to take part in such heroic events?"

Bucky couldn't believe what he was hearing. "What the hell kind of country does Klepakov think he's going to create?"

"A rich and noble nation, free of political obstructionists and biting flies of media."

He had the troubling sense that he'd heard the thousand-year speech once before, but it was pointless to bicker—Yuri was only the messenger. And remembering the kinkery that the oligarch relished with Knotty Natalie, he saw that he'd been right about something else: power and perversion were symbiotic. If Klepakov ever attained the control he sought, British politics would likely become a far more twisted business.

In the morning the Devi Way protesters failed to show, and all mention of International Fulfillment disappeared overnight from their website. Whatever their Boss had set in motion had hit hard, and fast. At noon a startling e-mail arrived from Sangita Sharma, who had somehow turned up his personal address; she proposed a meeting on a public street in Kensington. With Beard's advice still echoing, and uncertain what the oligarch's thugs had done to compel Sharma's quick retreat, he agreed to face his antagonist.

In a curt reply, she instructed him to meet her on Thurloe Place, between the Victoria & Albert Museum and the Brompton Oratory. He didn't know the spot, but he found his way from South Kensington Tube station. Oddly, Sharma was waiting for him before a statue of John Henry Cardinal Newman.

She raised her hand toward the statue as he approached. "It wasn't your name so much as your circumstances that made me think of this."

"Come again?"

"Surely you know that Newman converted from the Anglican faith to Catholicism? His entire world view changed at the age of forty-four, and led to the revitalization of the Roman church in England. The point is that men can change their minds, even about their deepest beliefs, and that can make a difference in the world."

Bucky was utterly lost. "Why would I know anything at all about that guy?"

"Well, apart from the name, you are a Catholic. At least that is what you wrote on the application for your first work permit, under Religious Affiliation."

He felt his bile rise at this latest breach of his privacy, and he nearly shouted, *How did you get your hands on that document?* But he was determined not to show weakness, reminding himself that Sharma had already proven a startling ability to dig and discover. "Even if that's true, I didn't come here to talk about theology."

"There is far more to it than abstract doctrine. In the sixteenth century a man with an equal lust for power and an heir closed the monasteries and trampled the Church in this country. I feel a certain hostility toward men who use women like breeding stock and then lop off their heads. And I take pleasure from the fact that John Henry Newman—the man who overturned Henry VIII's designs after three hundred years—was celibate from the age of fifteen. It's not often that life serves up an irony quite so satisfying."

"You didn't ask me here for a history lesson. What the hell do you want?"

"Walk with me, this way," Sharma said enigmatically. She strode off to the north with purposeful little steps, past the silent Oratory and into the bustle and noise of the shopping district on Brompton Road. It was a clear day, cool and brilliant, with a river breeze that swept the vehicle exhaust and invisible particles of dirt from the air. "I had hoped to shut down this glorified Bibighar you call International Fulfillment. But I understand that Devi Way does not have the power to overcome every adversary, especially one as callous as Klepakov."

"If he threatened to harm you, I'm sorry. It's beyond my control."

Sharma uttered a dismissive *huh*! "You would be amazed how often men say that, as if some puppet master pulls their strings."

"Our choices are limited. You're either a fucker or a fuckee in this world, a one or a zero. And I'm not going back to being a zero."

"What you're doing amounts to neither a one nor a zero.

If you insist on reducing your life to a number, it would be correctly stated as negative. And as I told you on the first day we met, it is a shameful waste. I have seen your work history. You have genuine talent. You should put it to better use."

Bucky didn't answer; he was still trying to work out why Sharma and her troublesome charity had backed down so fast after their opening attacks. They were approaching Harrods, and she motioned for them to cross the street toward the imposing storefront.

As they arrived at the first doorway she told him, "Follow me inside. There is something I want to show you." She led him toward the rear of the sprawling ground level, past cosmetics and jewelry counters, through an archway into a larger, altogether different space. "Men believe the best thing in life is sex—" she said in an abrupt shift.

"And you think it's love?"

"No, love is vital, but my mother always told me that only food can be counted on to bring joy each day, at every stage of life."

Bucky regarded her skeptically. "That's rating it too highly."

"You say that because you have always had your fill, and because you don't know what is possible. But look around you." Before them in the food courts lay a city block of gustatory delights—a fish and clam grill and oyster bar, a *fromagerie* and charcuterie, a caviar case and a steak house displaying the finest cuts of angus beef, an Italian trattoria and an ornamental sushi bar. They navigated around brightly hued pyramids of chocolates and truffle candies, crossed over mountains of tea, wandered through a wine room stacked with rare vintages and past a counter where glass-and-brass tubes like organ pipes offered columns of coffee beans. The pooled aromas of lamb, ham, chicken, venison, mushroom, steak and kidney pies swirled about their heads. The halls sparkled with jewel-like pastries and great heaps of sweet biscuits, dried fruits and nuts, olives in miniature oaken buckets, Moroccan, Indian, and Lebanese delicacies, puddings and sweet deserts.

The choice was overwhelming, but she made it for them. "What I really want is ice cream." She led him to a fountain with chromed revolving seats, where soda makers punched the buttons of blenders and scooped gelato or sorbet from rows of rounded paper tubs. They sat and opened menus.

"My mother was born in western India, the ninth of fourteen children. Food was not something one took for granted in Gujarat, much less banana splits…her parents were unschooled and dependent on a plot of worn-out land. She had more sisters than brothers, so when she reached the age of twelve, her father adjusted the balance by selling her to the agent of a brothel in Mumbai. It was a sensible act that fed the family for many months."

"That's a tough situation." Bucky was uncertain what else he could offer.

"I'll have Kulfi ice cream and a smidgen of the pudding," she said to the waiter. Bucky pointed to a tub at the opposite extreme of the cold case. "Strawberry."

"At your end of the trade there is no awareness of what it means to be a sex slave. Imagine yourself confined within a tiny room and ruled over by a master whose whims are law. All education comes to an end, apart from the practical things you may learn from elder prostitutes. And every moment of your time belongs to the master, who may permit men to use you at any hour, even day and night without pause during festivals and holidays. There will be no more days at play, nor trips to market or the riverbank or even outside the walls of the brothel. The master fears that his valuable slaves may flee his embrace, so every door is locked and guarded by men with sharpened weapons."

The waiter returned with their ice cream, and Bucky slipped a spoon inside the edge of his dish, not yet tasting it. "If that happened to your mother, it's awful. But it doesn't have anything to do with me."

"Naturally that is what you want to believe! But I promise, you have a vital role in this story. I will spare you the details of the beatings, the rapes, the sicknesses, the times when other young women in the brothel, who had become my mother's only friends, were sold on or died from maltreatment. It is enough to say that millions of girls are lost to slavery in India and a hundred other countries, and that perhaps one in a thousand manages to escape. But my mother was that one."

"How?"

"When she was sixteen and a blossom of beauty, she came to know a young man from a wealthy family. He wore elegantly tailored clothing, and his hair was always washed. He would even bathe before his visits. When he graduated from university, he was awarded a scholarship for further study in London. My mother had lain with him many times, and had done her utmost to please him and bind him to her. She told him that if he bought her passage to England, she would sleep on a mat in his kitchen and have sex with him whenever he wanted. He promised that he would find a way to bring her to England, but she sensed that he would not. So she allowed herself to become pregnant with his child."

Sharma paused to spoon some ice cream from her dish, wiping her small mouth with a napkin before continuing. Her movements were precise and fastidious, perfect table manners. "The day came when he visited her for the final time, and she pressed him about taking her to England. He turned cold and said it was impossible. Then she told him that she was carrying his child, and she was certain it was a boy. If he did not remove her from the brothel, the master would call for the abortion-ist as soon as her pregnancy was noticed. And unless she ran from India, the master's men would hunt her down and drag her back. She pleaded to be allowed to care for the boy, once they were safe in England. She vowed to devote her life to his nurturing. So the proud young man—who desired his first son, even from a whore—put her on a freighter to Liverpool, while he flew on to London. When she arrived, he wired her money for the train to Ilford. She worked there as a dishwasher until the night that I was born.

"Naturally my father was furious at being deceived. He slapped my mother and swore it was an evil thing to trick him, and that he would never acknowledge a poor unwanted girl. Indeed, he never has! But with an infant in her arms, my mother stood before a British immigration panel and pleaded not to be returned to the brothel in Mumbai. They allowed her to remain in this country."

Bucky sat in silence for a while before speaking. "You still haven't told me why you called off your campaign against us. Did Klepakov's people threaten you?"

She shook her head. "They offered me a cash donation of five thousand pounds. Their only conditions were that our pro-tests must end, and we must never expose your lofty oligarch nor any of your members. They also assured me that if I refused to accept their money, my mother would disappear."

Bucky wanted to offer some consolation, but the words just wouldn't come.

Sangita drew closer, speaking softly. "Do you see it now? As long as you eat from the crocodile's table, his crimes are truly your own."

ELEVEN

The disconsolate walk back to Belgrave Square gave him time to come to terms with the truth—his income, his liquor and food, even the bed in which he lay all fell like trinkets from Klepakov's hand. And his profitable new career had come with a caveat: he could not pretend to stand at any moral distance from the oligarch. Sangita Sharma had been right to lump him together with the hired goons who had threatened her mother's life. And yet earlier, standing before the Newman statue, she had suggested that he might be capable of rethinking his deepest beliefs. The whole business of the two Newmans—the cardinal and the computer wizard—had left him thoroughly confused. The two men couldn't have been more different, one focusing his life's energy on a quest for spiritual grace, the other directing equal energy toward the technical means to military triumph. Both had changed history, yet their lives were conceptual opposites, and seemed irreconcilable.

Yuri was waiting when he arrived at the house. "In view of recent troubles and connected expense, Nicolai Vasilievitch will increase his revenue share to fifty percent."

Bucky turned away. A reduction in his weekly cash flow seemed meaningless when weighed against the threat to Sangita's mother. He replayed her story in an endless loop, imagining the smell of fear in the Mumbai slave house, the frantic urge to escape, a seasick voyage, and then the life of an emigrant sex worker washing dishes to feed a daughter. Like unwelcome houseguests, the images refused to depart, prodding him to explore the world of abuse that Sangita had revealed. After an hour online he realized that the stories had been all around him for years, but somehow they had never left a lasting impression. Nepalese girls as young as ten were routinely sold into slavery. Philippine tour operators promised their punters sick "preteen adventures." In the brothels of North Africa genital mutilation was required for employment. He had never imagined himself being tied to anything remotely akin to these wrongs, but now, as the larger context came into view, he understood why the Devi Way flyer had called him out as just another victimizer.

He read more and thought it over for three days, weighing his evident guilt against an inner reluctance to see himself as a monster. Whatever the evidence against him might prove, he simply didn't *feel* evil. Finally, needing to talk it through, he emailed Sharma, asking if he could visit her office and women's shelter. She replied with an Ilford address that he recognized from the charity's website, adding, "*Come tomorrow.*"

Devi Way was reached only after a tiring walk from the rail station, east of the drab commercial High Street. The sky was thick and threatening to rain and in the ashen light the intersecting streets offered up brief, haunting vignettes of empty rail yards and the skeletal frameworks of drained petroleum tanks. At a greater distance, the weatherworn bell towers of Anglican and Methodist churches spiked above the rooftops. He passed a newly built gurdwara, then further down an older mosque; along the uneven sidewalks Muslim women in black *abayat* and *niqāb* sailed past like silent dhows. The air reeked of choking exhaust and syrupy Asian sauces, sweet floral perfumes and pungent body odors. Through the open doorways of Montego Chicken, Medina Market, and Mahima Sarees came voices speaking in exotic tongues. Until that day he had avoided the boroughs beyond the East End, but he had a strange sense of knowing the place in which he found himself. A grim dreariness hung upon it all, heavy padlocks securing the doors, yet the streets bustled with energy—life soldiered on here amid the gloom. He turned onto a side street lined with aging cars, its gutters littered with discarded food wrappers. In that moment he knew what had seemed familiar. It reminded him of Buffalo.

A hundred meters down, Sharma's charity occupied a dilapidated storefront with flats on the upper levels. A sign nailed to the outer door proclaimed, "Devi Way—Setting Spirits Free," above an image of the goddess Durga locked in battle, her many arms brandishing a shield, a scimitar, and a conch shell horn. He felt a stab of anxiety, wondering if Sangita would introduce him to her staff as "the swine behind the outrage at International Fulfillment." He reminded himself that they had been peaceful so far; they were unlikely to jump up and pummel him. Inside he found a ragged group of volunteers, some recognizable as the demonstrators who had besieged the house. They labored at metal tables piled high with newspaper clippings, notated maps, and battered twentieth-century computers. The room was inadequately lighted and not much warmer than the street, and smelled vaguely of fried fish and curry.

Sangita motioned to him from a doorway at the back of the space, beckoning him into a cramped and cluttered room with a secondhand desk and two folding chairs. Against the wall a floor-to-ceiling bookcase was heavily burdened with hardcover texts and academic paperbacks. He glanced at the titles as she toed the door shut behind him: *Philosophies of Social Science; Social Justice Without Socialism.*

She looked at him indifferently. "Why are you here? Tell me the real reason."

"I've been doing some reading—"

"Generally speaking that wouldn't do you any harm."

"You asked for a straight answer, just let me give it. I understand now what you're fighting. Maybe I can help. Maybe even pull the rug out from under these pricks."

"And destroy a competitor or two in the process. How clever…and it conveniently allows you to avoid the question of your own involvement."

Bucky took on the first part. "It's not about competition. It's their arrogance I can't stand. I've seen it too many times, in different fields. If I take them down a peg, the bastards list on your website might get a little shorter. If nothing else it would improve the page layout."

She ignored his final dig, responding, "A bastards list indeed! But take care, these aren't the sort of people who stand for any messing about. And the less I know about what you're doing, the better it is for Devi Way."

Something else had been bothering him. It seemed like the perfect moment to throw it back in her face. "Listen, one more thing—I checked out Vlad the Impaler. He turned twenty thousand people into human popsicles. Just how many acts of genocide do you think that I've committed?"

"I never accused you of genocide," she said without emotion.

"But you think I'm no better than the criminals on your website, don't you? Can we agree that I'm not a mass murderer? Would you give me that, at least?"

Sangita scowled and drew a long, irritated breath through her nostrils. "I suppose so. But since we're bargaining over your worth as a man, can we can also agree that what you have done here in London is nothing to be proud of?"

He hesitated, reaching for a sharp comeback, then saw that she had trapped him rhetorically. "I never said I was proud."

"You didn't need to. I saw it in your eyes, the day we first met. But I don't see it now."

He thought he might do better by shifting the blame, if not the topic. He recalled Klepakov's threats and the bribe that had been paid. "I know it's a filthy way to come by money, but maybe that contribution will do some good at your shelter. Is that what you have in mind?"

"I'm not going to discuss our plans for the oligarch's cash. Our programs are costly. There is never enough funding."

"I can imagine."

"I doubt that you can. You would need to see the shelter before you can possibly understand. It's not far, we can walk." She jumped to her feet and went out the door as if Bucky's consent were irrelevant.

He saw no point in refusing, and allowed himself to be led into the street and farther along the shabby road. "What about the municipal shelters? I read that the boroughs all have them. Why don't you just rely on that system?"

"Try finding a spot in any of them on a weekend night, when every woman in London with a drunken husband is desperate to avoid her next beating. Beds are always scarce. When we began trying to help the sex workers, we realized that many were literally sleeping in their brothels. We couldn't put them up in our homes or pay for hotels. We hatched the idea of building a shelter, and asked the boroughs for assistance, but all of them said it would be preferable if we located our facility in another part of London, or better yet, some far-off region of Scotland or Wales. No doubt they saw us as harebrained dilettantes."

He couldn't let go of the argument they'd been having; it had ended too quickly for his liking. A tenacious inner voice whispered that he could win if he pressed his case. "Do you understand that the morality of sex comes down to consent?"

"What? Are you mad?"

"You have to understand, I've never forced anyone to do anything. And where's the harm if it's all consensual? Do you really believe that a man paying a woman to have sex with him—and the woman taking the money—is some heinous human rights abuse? Both the punter and the girl get what they want, and the income allows her to enjoy whatever else she wants. I don't see what's wrong with that."

"Yes, I can see that the proposition appeals to you greatly. So how many of the women in your club have *you* paid to sleep with?"

"None of them! It's not what I'm into."

"Then are you one of those brutes who likes to bind and gag his women, or cane them for your sadistic pleasure?"

"No, and I'm not a pedophile or a sheep fucker or a flasher in a ratty overcoat. And since we're getting personal, what about you? Do you think that every sexual act outside of a consecrated marriage is a mortal sin? I've known Catholic priests who dipped their wicks more often than they prayed the Rosary. Maybe you need to get out more."

At this she blushed a scarlet shade, and Bucky felt a glow of satisfaction at managing to embarrass her.

Her voice quavered as if she had been physically struck. "Mock me if you wish, I do not care. But you would do far better to ponder your own dilemma."

Before he could respond, they turned onto a curving side lane, passed some ramshackle houses, then stopped abruptly before a low, rusting iron gate. Behind it stood a battered brick dwelling with a sagging roof. The gate creaked with age and corrosion as Sangita pushed through. They approached the door, where she knocked lightly in what sounded like a known pattern. "Wait while I get Mrs. McKenzie to open up. Some of our residents are afraid of being snatched back by their pimps. I try never to alarm them."

Bucky took it all in, trying to maintain a neutral expression. The yard was barren of greenery apart from two or three starving shrubs; the heavy limestone entry step had split through from front to back, the gap covered over by a stained fiber mat. In the window to their left a pane was broken out, the jagged gap patched with cardboard wrapped in plastic. Crumbling mortar fell from the bed joints of the brickwork, and a closer look revealed that the once-smooth surfaces of the bricks had been pockmarked by a billion raindrops.

The door opened slightly, to the limit of a substantial chain. "No worries, it's only me, with a visitor."

The chain disappeared and the door fell back. In the foyer stood a stocky woman with suspicious eyes. She sized up Bucky as if she were deciding whether to brain him with a rolling pin, then, satisfied that he presented no threat, she stood aside, securing the door behind them when they had entered. Wooden floorboards groaned beneath their feet—the oak planks had curled up at the edges from water damage, all traces of varnish long since scuffed away. Overhead, yellow stains oozed along the ceiling lines, and random cracks meandered down the plaster walls toward the ruined floor.

They advanced into a lounge at the front of the house. Two women reclined on a tattered couch, one of them flicking cigarette ash into a paper cup, the other nursing a cold. For a moment, Bucky thought he was dreaming—the smoker bore an uncanny resemblance to Mandy. But with a closer look, the suntanned skin and dazzling teeth of the Australian beauty became only pallor and dull decay. She sensed his disapproval and quickly got up and retreated into the interior of the shelter; the other girl pulled a wad of tissue from her pocket and blew her nose with a phlegmy honk. On the far wall three unframed female images had been fixed with tape. Bucky recognized Indira Ghandi in the middle photograph, but the outer figures were unknown to him. Sangita seemed taken aback when he asked their identities, as if he'd been baffled by a bust of Admiral Nelson or the Duke of Wellington. "To the left is Meerabai, the mystical singer. To the right, Girija Devi, savior of the untouchables of Bihar. Our charity takes its name from her."

A boiler clanked beneath their feet, and the wall radiators hissed; from the upper floor came the cries of an angry baby, its tiny voice filled with rage. "Wait here," Sangita said. She climbed the stairs, careful to announce herself, then after a few moments she called out from above, directing him to follow her to the second level. He went up reluctantly. She stood beside a changing table in a cramped bedroom. To her left was a pale slight woman of no more than nineteen.

"I want you to experience something that will change your perspective on all of this. Surely you know how to change a nappy?"

Bucky hadn't expected to find an infant in the shelter, and he gaped in disbelief, wanting any excuse to refuse. "It's all right, sir, she won't mind," said the adolescent mother. He didn't want to offend her, but he couldn't seem to move his legs.

"You're not afraid, are you?" Sangita mocked him with her eyes as much as her tone.

He forced himself to step forward and begin unpinning the soiled paper wrap; a bitter stench assaulted his nostrils, and he turned his head. As he recoiled, the baby girl shifted on the table, and a dark and curving lozenge fell over the edge and across the toe of his shoe. He couldn't contain himself, "Damn it! This is the worst—"

"This is *nothing*," Sangita said harshly. "Finish what you're doing. When you're done, I want you to meet Mary Rose."

Bucky cleaned and diapered the girl and handed her back to her mother, then, after wiping his tainted shoe, followed Sangita into another room. Inside, a woman lay in shadows on a narrow bed, the single floor lamp darkened. She raised herself up slowly, clutching her ribs on one side. Sangita flicked the lamp to life, illuminating her bruised face and involuntary tremors.

"Are you feeling any better? I have more of the pills the doctor prescribed, if you are still in pain."

"It's not so bad as before, miss."

"This is Mr. Newman. He is here to learn about our shelter. Why don't you tell him how you came to us?"

The injured woman gathered herself, drawing a few shallow breaths until she had wind enough in her lungs. "There's a house out by Luton, beyond the airport. Not your posh sort of place like central London, they cater to the more disgusting types, if you get my meaning. Our minder was Hanif. He wasn't a big man, but he carried a cricket bat. God we were terrified! When I tried to get away he did this to my ribs. The second time I ran, I managed to flag down a police car. I told them what went on at the house, and they wrote it all down before they dropped me off at hospital. They only let you stay so long in the wards, and the borough shelter was chock-full. The discharge clerk gave me this address, and enough money for the train and a taxi from the station. I'm grateful for the bed."

Bucky said nothing about the complaint to the police; he assumed they had been handsomely paid to bury it. Outside the room, Sangita took hold of his arm with a fierce grip, whispering into his ear, "A bit different than the Belgravia high life, isn't it?"

Once more he was stumped for a retort. They descended the stairs and went out into the street, pacing back to the Devi Way office under a spitting rain and a cloud of uncomfortable silence. At the corner, as they waited to cross, Sangita took him by surprise again, asking in her matter-of-fact way, "Do you want to have children?"

The phrasing made it sound as if she were asking him to father *her* children, and he stared blankly, unable to respond. The thought of starting a family couldn't have been further from his mind. In the months since International Fulfillment had opened, no child had entered the house, and nothing inside the paneled walls would have allowed an alien to conclude that juvenile humans even existed.

"That's not possible, not until I'm older. Forty, maybe, who knows?"

Sangita shook her head, the lines around her mouth widening into disdain. "You have been living in a cage for exotic birds. The world must welcome and nurture children or cease to exist. Can you not see that?"

"Of course, but you need a steady income, a house with a yard, the right schools—"

She cut him off. "You know the circumstances of my birth. None of what you describe was present, and yet my mother has told me that the greatest joy of her life was bringing me into this world. Do you think she would take it back? Do you think I would wish away my own existence? Life is much stronger than the little things you fear."

They fell into silence again, until he spoke up as they passed a derelict betting parlor. "That woman, Mary Rose…find out everything you can about the people who hurt her. Names, addresses, phones, websites, business entities, bank accounts, whatever you can get. Then contact me."

"What are you going to do?"

"I thought you didn't want to know."

At the charity office, Bucky thanked her impersonally for the tour of the shelter, expecting a curt "Pleasure, good-bye!" in return. But Sangita stood in the doorway as if she were reluctant to part. "I live upstairs with my mother. This is the neighborhood where I spent my childhood. What do you think of our corner of England?"

"It reminds me of Buffalo, where I grew up."

Her changed expression gave her away—he had finally managed to astonish her. "Really? Like this? I would never have imagined."

■ ■ ■

Bucky's search for a point of attack began at the top of the Devi Way shit list. The first operation was not a single entity but a diverse conglomerate—a network of loose collaborators pumping out every profitable vice. One of their sites, Mayfair Mademoiselles, offered high-glam escorts in London, Paris, Rome, and Dubai. The pix were dazzling: stunning East European, Spanish and Italian girls, all Photoshopped to improbable perfection and available for in-call or outcall. A linked website within a different domain offered pay-per-minute HD porn and 24-7 webcams of naked teenagers, hard at work with their sex toys. Beneath this quasi-legal surface layer, Devi Way had uncovered a swamp of slave dens and street prostitution, and possibly the first meth lab in Britain. The same men controlled it all.

He understood that cutting off any one of the hydra's heads would only cause it to grow back double. But if he could touch off a battle between the people at the top, they might destroy each other.

"I'll blow your house down," he said to his monitor, and then—for the first time in his life—he put on the Black Hat and went to war.

He hacked the Mayfair Mademoiselles web server and burrowed deeply into their files, scanning thousands of lines of code, searching for chinks in the armor. Even as his eyes passed over blocks of JavaScript and strings of applets and database calls, he kept seeing a young woman's damaged face within the code. He worked through the night, developed an approach, crafted some malicious files. An hour before dawn he uploaded a concealed redirect to the Mayfair Mademoiselles server. His script sent the click-throughs from their banner ads to the porn & webcams site instead, pirating the traffic of the escorts operation. The simple tactic had the unmistakable stink of an inside job.

Next he concealed two ingenious scripts within the billing forms for the porn and webcams site. The first caused every credit card charge to be double-billed; the second reversed any attempted refund, logging instead a third unauthorized charge against the customer's card. He wrapped this plot with a further deception. Rather than disguising his initial penetration with a rootkit, he spoofed his IP to make it look like a clumsy hack from within the Mayfair Mademoiselles domain. The unknown boss of each operation would conclude that the other man was trying to ruin him. Bucky's only regret was that he couldn't watch them come to blows.

He had never expected it to feel so good—he was dealing out e-justice to insolent turds, with all the juvenile joy of a Halloween vandal smashing pumpkins. Yet as he pictured himself running the list, savaging Devi Way's enemies, a strange spirit of redemption fell over him. As a boy, he had been taught to reject the false concept of salvation through good works, but if he hosed off the scum from Sangita Sharma's list, he thought it might improve her assessment of his life. He didn't see it as a penance—it was too much fun to be part of any search for forgiveness—but it had the quality of a moral realignment.

Over the days that followed he waged an escalating cyber war. He launched a worm into the Deep Web that conjured a vast botnet of corrupted machines, slaved to his control, then triggered crushing denial-of-service attacks against the sleaziest web rings. He hacked the British credit bureaus and destroyed the personal ratings of pedophile filmmakers and snide brothel keepers. He ravaged the live teenie-cam websites, deleting all their customer logons, then infected their servers with a military virus that shut down cooling fans and spun the hard drives furiously until they burst into flames.

When a pair of pimps in Birmingham diversified into counterfeit pharmaceuticals, he unleashed his malware masterpiece: a false flag ransomware attack against their chief supplier. He punched through the firewall in front of the supplier's e-commerce engine and injected code that would splash lurid porn across their screens whenever they accessed their orders queue. As the hard-core JPEGs faded, the merchants would see a terrifying ultimatum—apparently from the Birmingham duo—"Pay us £10,000 via cash-by-text transfer, or this program will erase your business records." He laughed to tears as he imagined the low-tech panderers trying to work out what had happened, and why their prime source of chemicals was suddenly screaming death threats.

Each electronic victory made him bolder and hungrier for targets. Devi Way had done a laudable job of turning up felons, but they were scratching the surface. If you wanted to know what went on in real time—where the hidden sex dens and the kiddie parlors were setting up for business that week—you had to lurk in private chat rooms. Unlike the legal porn purveyors or the high-end escort ops, the bottom-feeders avoided the web, relying on social media. He spent hours following their cryptic tweets and group IMs, picking up clues, noting patterns. When "Wormwood" was mentioned three times in one week by different punters, he knew he'd found something that even Sangita and her people had missed. It took another week to pry loose a phone number for the house in Wormwood Scrubs, from a punter in a chat room. But that unlocked a hidden door.

When he called, pretending interest, the voice on the other end of the line sounded oddly familiar, but he dismissed it, telling himself that all East European accents sounded more or less alike. The woman who answered had the same reaction. "Have we met before? I don't remember your name, Mr. Farquhar, but your voice sounds…never mind, it doesn't matter. We can accommodate almost any fetish or bizarre pleasure, the only limit is your own imagination. The prices vary accordingly, but then a gentleman such as yourself will know that."

He booked an hour appointment at the Wormwood Scrubs house, then typed the address the madam provided into an online maps page. It came up as a winding side street near Du Cane Road, not far beyond Her Majesty's Prison. The Tube station to which she directed him was close at hand—in spite of their low profile, whoever was behind the Wormwood house had chosen a location where men could come and go with ease, and in numbers.

He planned to scope the house from the street, maybe snap a few photos with his phone. He had no concept yet of how he might undermine their operation, but it seemed logical that his first step should be to get eyes on the property. When the afternoon came, his first impression was of insignificance. The house appeared no different from any of the brick-and-stucco structures in the residential blocks to the west of the prison. Dented cars and muddy tradesmen's vans had been driven up onto the sidewalks, the wheels on one side hunkering down over the curbs. He slipped behind a vehicle opposite the house and captured two quick pictures of an unremarkable two-story, with curtains blanketing every window. He felt a wave of indecision—was it all a waste of time? Then he decided that he couldn't turn and leave; he had to go in, to learn what he could before making some excuse and exiting.

His knock brought a sallow-faced young woman with a lawnmower haircut and a broken left bicuspid. "I'll just get Mrs. Sandringham for you," she said, using the madam's improbable name. She extended her hand toward a red velour sofa. "Do make yourself comfortable." Bucky remained on his feet instead, his heart beginning to pound. He was learning nothing. The whole exercise was stupid. Whatever kinkiness went on inside was well concealed; to get past the anteroom would require him to name his pleasure and pay in advance. He moved for the door, intending to run, then heard the same familiar voice calling out from the hallway, approaching as she spoke. "Mr. Farquhar, is that you?" As she entered the room, everything made sickening sense. It was Marie-Chantal.

He recognized her first, in spite of the ten kilos she had packed on since their meeting at the Ritz. "You *are* Mr. Farquhar, aren't you?" she asked with an artificial smile. Then with her own moment of recognition, she threw up her hands and cried, "Help, *help*! It's the wanker, *the wanker*!"

He slowed from a full-on sprint only as East Acton Tube station came into view. A policeman stood outside the entrance. It wouldn't be wise to approach at a run. He thought that no one had pursued him as he bolted from the house, ducking between the rows of cars to cover his escape. But before boarding a Central Line train he slipped into the fetid station toilet, where he turned his jacket inside out and donned a pair of sunglasses.

TWELVE

Laira interrupted him the following morning as he slogged through bills and payroll. A young East Indian woman was at the door, insisting on speaking with him. Was he perhaps away for the day? Bucky told her that he would see the unexpected visitor. He shuffled into the Entry Hall and released the latch—Sangita Sharma stood on the step, her eyes hot with rage.

"You fool! You could have been beaten up, or worse. What were you thinking, going out there alone?"

For a moment he wanted to hit back, *How the hell do you know anything about it?* But by now it was obvious that nothing escaped her. "What makes it any of your business?"

"I warned you not to mess about with these people. You were lucky. Next time might be different."

Her fists were tightly clenched at her sides, her lower lip trembling; she appeared to have made the journey from Ilford to Belgrave Square solely to vent. They had spoken their minds, but it seemed wrong to turn her away from the door so quickly.

"At this time of day it's just me and our greeter. Don't stand there freezing."

Sangita held back—the idea of entering the house was clearly repugnant. But the morning was chill and damp, and shivering, she stepped across the polished threshold. Bucky offered to take her coat, but she refused, either craving the warmth or unwilling to signal that she would stay more than moments. She turned toward the credenza by the stairs—eyes wide at the codpiece collection—then gazed upward, revolving to take in the columned magnificence of the hall, with its erotic frescoes and bronze-over-plaster medallions.

"Cupid, Venus, Bacchus, Hymen. My God, the impudence of it! Is it all like this, a tasteless phallic fantasy?"

"I'm not responsible for the architecture," Bucky protested. "And there are more comfortable rooms. I'll get you something warm to drink." He led her into the Library, seating her at an Italian Renaissance reading table with an inlaid mosaic after Botticelli. He went out briefly to find Laira, and asked her to bring tea.

When he returned, Sangita was studying the table intently. "Do you realize that at auction this would bring a full year's income for the average Londoner?"

"Maybe more, the oligarch poured in millions. People like him spend as much as they want. It's just the way life works."

"Yes, you explained it all so elegantly, 'fuckers and fuck-ees.' I wonder which one I am."

"I didn't mean to imply—"

"*Please*, I wasn't looking for an answer."

Laira arrived with a silver tea service and two bone china cups and saucers. The moment she had put down the tray, Bucky thanked her and told her that he would serve; she made no effort to hide her Mona Lisa smile as she left the room. He drew Sangita's cup toward his side of the tray and poured from the weighty silver teapot, recalling the image of Amelia Wax filling her younger sister's cup. He tried to serve as perfectly as the ten-year-old.

"About that business yesterday…up until now it's all been remote intrusions. But these people were flying under the radar. I had to go out there and see for myself."

She lifted her cup and drank, appearing to take strength from the hot lemon tea. Laira had brought shortbreads, and Sangita quickly swallowed two of them, then, more slowly, a third. "There have been wild rumors flying about, tales of hacking and high-level trickery. Someone has been causing a great deal of trouble for the people that we scrutinize."

"*Someone?*"

"I should have known!"

"You asked me to keep you out of it. I have."

"But you must understand that Devi Way could fall under suspicion. If these criminals think that we are to blame for your electronic attacks, they might take their revenge. I have already been threatened once. You must exercise the greatest care from now on."

"What about that house in Luton?" Bucky changed the subject slightly. "Have you learned anything more?"

She had finished her tea, and he refilled her cup. "We have confirmed that at least a dozen women either live in the house, or come and go. Hanif, the guard that Mary Rose mentioned, has been observed entering and leaving, but there are others too. Rough men. We are not able to confront a group like that. We don't have the strength."

A difficult silence lasted until Bucky said, "Would you like to see the rest of the club?"

"I have seen quite enough." She got up and made for the door. Going out into the cold, she paused for a moment, then said offhandedly, "You know you don't belong here."

His anger flashed. "What, in Britain?"

"No, not Britain. This house. This life. I see a different future for you." Without waiting for a response, she turned and marched off toward the Tube.

Bucky spent the rest of the day rehashing the events since Sangita's first appearance—the street protests, the telephoto shots, the bullying payoff and uneasy truce, then his own secret war against Devi Way's multiple enemies. He couldn't be certain whether the storm had passed harmlessly or had inflicted hidden damage. When the blurb about their club was removed from the Devi Way website, he dismissed it as a tiny thorn, soon plucked out, and assumed that no one had noticed the listing or their eye-popping address. But later that week a newspaper reporter in a trench coat and turtleneck knocked at the door. He flashed an electronic pass with his photo and his paper's logo, and asked for a comment on the exposé of International Fulfillment that would run in their Sunday edition.

"There's no story here, and I have nothing to say."

The hard-bitten reporter wasn't about to be put off. He drew a notebook from his coat, waving it like a summons. "Let me read to you what we intend to print, for any response you may wish to make. 'Within a private gentlemen's club in Belgrave Square, dripping with luxury and obscene excess, naked beauties cuddle and cavort with the wealthy and powerful of London. Reportedly, alcohol-fueled orgies of the most shocking nature run round-the-clock at this mischievous mansion. Knowledgeable sources confirm that any and all fantasies are indulged, even bondage and disci—'"

Bucky slammed the door and ran for Yuri. "We're going to be outed in one of the tabloids."

"Which paper?" his partner asked, apparently untroubled.

"The one with the red-and-white logo."

"*Da*, I know this rag, it is popular in working-class circles. Do not concern yourself."

"If the story runs, other outlets will pick it up."

Yuri spoke reassuringly. "I am great admirer of American inventions, but in matter of silencing rampant journalists, you must bow to superior Russian skills."

"You're going to intimidate the reporter?"

"No, *tovarish*. The publisher's banker, who is one of our members, will do that for us. You will excuse me while I make certain telephone calls?"

Days later, when the oligarch appeared for his latest smacker with Natalie, he first desired a private exchange. The request took Bucky by surprise; Klepakov rarely spoke to him, acknowledging his presence only with the occasional flippant wave. Through the trials of the previous weeks the oligarch's commands had come down through Yuri, but after the brush with the tabloid reporter, he had more to say, and this time directly. The customary henchmen accompanied him, prowling the corners of the Salon. Neither looked to be in an amiable mood.

"I will translate," Yuri said, readying himself. Klepakov launched into a personal version of a commissar's May Day oration, fat finger wagging like Khrushchev, grasping fist raised high like Lenin exhorting the lumpen. He snarled and raged, berated and bellowed, roaring his way through the unabridged list of filthy Russian oaths. Hearing the tirade, Jackie Wax slipped into the salon, eyes narrowing, casually shaking out his arms. He nodded to the hoodlums, but the Russian muscle knew his reputation. The older of the two coughed in some kind of signal to the younger man, who looked for a place to spit, then swallowed instead.

At last Klepakov worked up to a climax, raging at Bucky, "*Vy absolyutnyy pozor*, you fucking geek!" Panting hard, he motioned for the translation. Yuri inhaled and opened his mouth, but Bucky waved him off.

"Tell him I understood every word."

■ ■ ■

Sangita's gift for unearthing the truth soon manifested again. One morning as Bucky clawed his way toward consciousness with a strong Americano, a chat window popped open on his workstation monitor:

— *Are you awake?*

Discovering this latest ID hardly seemed worthy of mention; if Sangita announced that she had sequenced his DNA and found the defective genes, he would not have been shocked. But what she wanted next was completely unforeseen:

— *Yo, I'm here*

— *Thank you for receiving me at your club, and for your gracious hospitality*

— *It's nothing, forget about it*

— *Would you care to join my mother and me for dinner at our flat, on Thursday?*

He stared at the screen, amazed that Sangita could think that she owed him a return invitation. "Frickin' British manners!" he said in disbelief. Worse, he couldn't think of a way to turn her down without looking like an ass. She posted another line before he could respond.

— *We cannot match the opulence of your club, but I promise my mother's cooking will be excellent*

— *I can't make it*

— *Would another evening be more convenient for you?*

— *I can't make it*

— *I feel obligated to return your hospitality, but I cannot afford dinner at a restaurant*

Now he was sweating, wishing that he had ignored her first query; he couldn't bail out smoothly, but he thought of a way to throw her off. She had his e-mail and his chat ID, but not his phone number.

— *Call my mobile and we'll talk*

He closed the chat window to prevent her from asking for the number, then leaned back in his leather chair, assuming he was safe. Seconds later his cell rang. He didn't bother with hello, snapping, "Look, you told me your mother's story, and I'm sure you've told her all about me. How am I supposed to turn up for dinner when she sees me as one of the plague rats who destroyed her life?"

Sangita gasped at his rudeness. "I have told my mother only that you are an American who has helped Devi Way. She has no reason to fear or resent you."

Bucky refused again, even more coldly, but Sangita would not relent, pleading with him, "Will you not reconsider?"

He almost hung up without responding, then he recalled his visit to Wax's home, and how, to his amazement, the afternoon had turned out to be enjoyable. And Sangita's admission of poverty touched him. Reluctantly he agreed to come to Ilford for an evening.

Days later, when the door opened onto the smallest and most unadorned flat he had ever entered, he questioned his decision, wondering if there would be room for three adults to sit down to a meal. But if the living space above the charity office was painfully compact, at least Mukta Sharma was not the fiery critic he had feared. Before him stood a smiling soul with two golden teeth, in a green-and-aqua sari and a pair of purple Reeboks. She was an inch or two taller than her daughter and more than double her girth, and although she was no longer the beauty that Sangita had spoken of, from earlier times in Mumbai, Bucky had to admit that she was still a handsome woman. Mukta took his coat and welcomed him into her home; a strong but pleasant aroma filled the flat, a mix of spices and oils, and something like cooked lentils.

He held out a bottle. "I brought a chardonnay from the Finger Lakes region. You won't see much from that appellation at Marks & Spencer."

Sangita accepted the wine, opened it, and filled two juice glasses from a breakfast set. "My mother does not drink alcoholic beverages. Normally I have only a little, but since it is special I will join you."

Mukta returned to her stove, where pots simmered. Mysterious dishes baked in the oven below. In the confinement of the tiny flat, the living room and dining room were one, and that room was undivided from the kitchen—anywhere they stood, the three of them were all but pressed together. The walls were bare apart from Sangita's framed diploma and a photograph of the Taj Mahal, scissor-cut from a magazine; below it, on an unsteady wooden table, stood a bronze of the dancing Shiva. An earthenware dish held a burning incense cone.

"I know you are American," Mukta began, "but little else. Did you study at university?"

"Call me Bucky, and yes, I studied computer science at Buffalo. I worked in IT for five years in New York, before coming to London."

"There are many young people in India who have taken up computer work. It is certainly much easier on the back than farming or weaving. Do you work on big computers? I have heard that some are massive."

"I use a laptop for anything that I can't get done with a phone. For the most part, the big computers are in the cloud."

Mukta appeared to find this completely logical. "I see, there are several airports in London. That must be important for you, to reach those great machines. I would be afraid of so much flying. Are you a religious practitioner?"

Bucky was caught off guard by her question about his beliefs, but he answered before Sangita could intervene. "I was brought up as a Roman Catholic, that was my mother's faith. But I don't attend Mass…at least I haven't since arriving here."

Mukta nodded her understanding. "There are many Catholic churches in England. I am sure they would take you back, if you asked politely. And I have always liked Jesus, he is one of the most interesting emanations of Lord Krishna. Have you read the Bhagavad-Gita?"

He started to ask, *Who?* but Sangita cut off the exchange. "Bucky was born in a city where the snowfall exceeds the Himalayas. I have read that in Buffalo, snow blankets rows of automobiles and even covers small houses."

Bucky realized that after his casual comparison of Ilford and Buffalo, she must have researched the place of his birth. At least the facts she trotted out were harmless—she could have dredged up far more embarrassing material. "That's true. Sometimes we had to jump out a second-floor window and shovel out the drifts that blocked the front door. It was nine or ten feet of accumulation."

"It is a wonder you could stay warm!" Mukta exclaimed. "What kind of food will grow in such a frozen land?"

Bucky had to think; he had never considered Buffalo to be an agricultural hub. "There are peach and apple orchards in western New York, maybe pumpkins, beans, some vegetables. I'm really not sure, I grew up on steaks and burgers like anybody else."

At this, Mukta's expression fell. "Oh, you slaughtered cattle? I did not know. I have prepared malai kofta, biryani, and palak paneer. I hope vegetarian food is acceptable?"

"It smells delicious." When Sangita moved to refill his glass, her let her pour until it brimmed.

"I am relieved. And do you prefer Peshwari naan or naan-parathas?"

Bucky didn't have a clue, but when the food came, he found it to be appetizing, even if he could not identify any course by name. Less palatable was Mukta Sharma's next tack:

"Did you know that Sangita is also a university graduate? She was a gifted student, and won a prize for the best essay on the transformation of the British welfare state."

"Please, Amma," Sangita begged, "no one is interested in my school assignments."

But Mukta was on a roll. "What is your view of our society? Does it seem to you that we are tolerant and just? Are you happy to be here in London, after living in New York?"

Bucky swallowed and took a sip of wine to clear his mouth. "I have no complaints. England has been fair enough to me."

To his left, Sangita rolled her eyes. As dinner concluded she whispered something to her mother, who covered a giggle and left the room. It smacked of a prearranged maneuver, but the whole evening could be written off that way. He expected Sangita would turn to personal questions, rummaging through his family history and making pointed inquiries about his parents, brothers, and sisters.

Instead she wanted to talk business. "I told you what we had learned about the house at Luton. Now there's more. At least six women, possibly eight or more, are being held against their will. And we have confirmed that the police are bribed to look the other way. If only we had the right people and vehicles, we would take matters into our own hands."

"Meaning what?"

"Come crashing in and pull the women right out of their cribs! Spirit them away by car and then to our shelter. Of course they will need time and counseling, and useful skills before they can hope for something better than filling the pockets of wicked men. Setting them free is just the beginning—but as I said, it's impossible."

Bucky weighed the consequences of his next step. "I know some men who may be able to help. One of them has a plumber's lorry. It's large enough for all of us and whoever else we might carry away."

"Are you sure these men can handle themselves? I can't look after any weak sisters."

"I think they'll hold up their end."

She considered his offer, stacking his assurances against her doubts. "All right, if you say so. Tell them to get ready. We're going on a raid."

THIRTEEN

"You're not heading out there on your own, guv'nor," Jackie Wax declared with a Guinness in hand when Bucky revealed their strategy. "What happens to me job if you're six feet under? And if I put in a word, Atkins and Rolle will likely sign on as well. As for Corporal Hobart and his lorry, I shall inquire and report back."

Overnight, Sangita had forwarded the address of the Luton house. Sizing up the property online, in street view, revealed nothing of any advantage; the usual rolling video cam had recorded only a featureless row house. The borough property records indicated company ownership, and the entity was registered, but no specific details turned up. That meant they would be going in blind. When Wax returned with Hobart's promise of the plumber's van, and confirmation that his brothers in arms would join him on the Luton raid, the operation was on. Bucky advised Sangita, who chose a date and time.

Through the upsets and alarms of the previous weeks, the club had motored smoothly along, steadily adding members and throwing off rising profits, compelling him to maintain a tight hold on the day-to-day. Yuri was little help—his attention had been diverted by some new oligarchic adventure. At first Bucky thought his partner was simply trying to regain the Boss's trust, shaken by the tabloid threat, but something more byzantine was in the works. Klepakov had begun hosting private meetings in the Library with a clutch of Russians and East Europeans, who came and went without introduction. Yuri had been drafted to act as gofer, hustling in and out with drinks and ice, delivering stacks of books on government and monetary history, even furnishing a balance scale borrowed from the kitchen. Once, a sound like coins jingling came from inside the chamber, followed by shouts—*Bravo, Nicolai Vasilievitch, bravo!* The posse emerged with Cheshire cat grins, heartily slapping each other's backs. Bucky welcomed anything that might lift Yuri's spirits, dashed by Fabiana's departure. But whatever the cause, Yuri kept it to himself.

He was not alone in making new plans; Natalie had been industrious too. "I'm launching an Internet film career," she confided over drinks in the Grand Saloon. "It might be a better opportunity than life in some dreary laboratory."

Bucky was caught off guard. "What about your PhD?"

She threw back her head with a laugh. "Oh, it will keep. But I've just put up a website, KnottyNatalie.net, and I'm working with the hottest fetish studio in London. We just shot five new B&D films—they're available pay-per-view or as downloads from my site. The money rolls in day and night. I'm earning more than a senior researcher."

To Bucky, the idea of giving up a doctoral program in the sciences for a career in fetish films was madness, and he opened his mouth to talk sense to Natalie. Then he recalled his own path. A part of him wanted to rail against her plans, and connect it to the evils that he had been fighting. But what she was doing was perfectly legal, and had nothing to do with the crimes that went on at Luton, or in a hundred other slave dens. So where did fetish cross over into felony? He wasn't sure he could say, precisely.

Natalie continued to brag up her efforts as she drained a martini. "My new site has a mobile app we call FoneLicks, and weekly webcam chats for subscription members. We're gearing up to sell live cam footage by the minute. I tried to approach it like a research project, and run all the permutations of channels and functions, but the *real* problem is zillions of competitors. I'm just a minnow in the online sea."

Now Bucky was on solid ground. "What are you doing to promote your site? Do you have a pay-per-click campaign or an affiliate marketing program? What about social media?"

Natalie frowned. "I don't have the budget for paid ads, but I have to do something that puts me on the map. Something splashy."

He extended his arms to encompass the house. "Suppose you didn't need Klepakov and your other clients? Would you concentrate full time on your film and web work?"

She swallowed the last of her drink. "I wouldn't mind giving up sessions here at the club. And seeing Kleppie twice a week is as boring as shopping for laundry soap. I want to be the number one submissive on the web, not the private toy of a lard-arsed oligarch with a spanking fetish." She took a sharp little bite of her olive. "You won't tell him I said that, will you?"

"I'll think about tactics and get back to you," Bucky promised before leaving the table. Walking away, he wondered how many British scientists would gladly give up their grants if some red-light website paid them double.

■ ■ ■

On the morning of the Luton raid, fog and rain blanketed the south of England. Bucky met Wax, Atkins, Rolle, and their driver Hobart at the Dartford train station; they slogged through the skidding traffic and onto the M25, crawling through the Dartford tunnel until they emerged a mile north of the Thames and began to struggle toward Ilford on the congested A road. At

Hobart's insistence, Bucky occupied the front passenger seat, with Wax and the other men crouching uncomfortably, knees drawn up, on the bare metal floor of the cargo area. Hobart had unloaded the bulk of his tools and supplies to free up more space, but the scents of faucet grease and thread-sealing compound lingered in the van. The rain worsened as they made the turn at Barking, beating down so intensely that the churning wiper blades barely allowed a forward view.

They found Sangita waiting just inside the Devi Way office, with the stout shelter matron, Mrs. McKenzie, and two older men whom Bucky remembered from the street protests at Belgrave Square. Despite huddling out of the rain they looked bedraggled and in need of a decent breakfast, or maybe stronger coffee. Wax, Atkins, and Rolle leaped from the back of the van, cursing the showers under their breath as they threw open the rear doors and called for everyone to pile in. Wax drew himself up and straightened his back, cramped by the ride—in his jump boots he towered over Sangita, standing half again her height.

"Who are you men?" she challenged.

Wax drew a maroon beret from under his belt and fitted it to his head with a grin. "Elements of the Air Assault Brigade."

"You're not carrying weapons? I won't have that kind of violence."

"We won't need 'em, miss, though me mate's probably got a pipe wrench in the lorry." At this, Atkins and Rolle broke out laughing.

Bucky had come around from the passenger side; he stood bareheaded in the rain, little rivulets coursing down his face. "I've got shotgun," he said to Sangita, instantly regretting the Americanism. "I hope it's not too rough in the back."

"So these are your men? Soldiers of fortune, are they?" But she hopped into the cargo bay and hunkered down beside Wax, who threw an arm over her shoulders and told her, "I have a daughter about your size." Bucky shut the doors behind the raiders and ran for the dry front seat.

At the Luton house they crept warily past the property, detecting nothing out of the ordinary. Parking was tight, and Bucky told Hobart to continue to the next intersection, then double back. Wax had come up to kneel between the two front seats, clutching the seat backs, sizing up the neighborhood. The rain didn't help. At the crossroads they awkwardly reversed course. From the far end of the lane—where they had entered moments before—a compact panel truck turned in and pulled up before the target house, blinkers flashing. The driver got out, opened the back, and removed an airline pet cage. He looked left and right suspiciously and then toted the plastic cage into the house.

Wax didn't like it. "What the hell? Push up, let's have a closer look." Hobart narrowed the distance, and after going past once more, he managed to slip the van into a space on the far side of the road.

"Listen to me, all of you," Sangita said with authority. "This is all about timing. We go in hard, we pull the women out, we get away as fast as we can."

They waited until the deliveryman emerged and drove off, then at Sangita's command they tumbled out of the van, leaving the rear doors spread wide. As they made for the house, Hobart called after them, "I'll be here with the engine running."

Bucky turned to reply but already Wax was through the gate and accelerating toward the house—he booted the front door and it ripped from the hinges, landing cocked against a wall in the entryway. He rushed inside, Atkins and Rolle close behind, with Sangita, Mrs. McKenzie, and the two older men at their heels. From inside, vile shouts rang out in response to the attack. Close behind, Bucky saw a great fat woman with flaming hair wobble toward them from an inner room, but at the sight of Wax she shrieked and ran the opposite way, overturning a table as she fumbled for a cell phone. Two swarthy men pushed past her and collided with the raiding party as it reached an open lounge. One of them seized a whisky bottle and hurled it at Atkins, who ducked as the missile flew past his head. Rolle leaped at the man and gut punched him, then scooped him up by his arm and ankle and sent him crashing through a window. The second goon was fool enough to swing at Wax, who walloped him so fiercely that the man's shoes flew off.

Sangita and her people swept past the melee, making for the bedrooms. "Rescue, rescue," Sangita shouted, banging the walls, "Everyone get out now!" As Atkins and Rolle kicked down the bolted doors, Mrs. McKenzie and Sangita charged into the cribs. Naked punters fell from the beds and grabbed for their pants and wallets, bleating with shock and sudden fear. An Asian girl in micro knickers shot from a chamber behind them and raced down the hallway. Mrs. McKenzie rousted an unclothed man from a bedroom, driving him out with an angry arse kick as she called to the girls, "Run to the plumber's lorry!"

Around them chaos and curses swirled—then from another room, Sangita cried for help. A girl lay chained to a metal bed, her wrists bound above her head and secured with a padlock.

"There's bolt cutters in the van," Wax shouted. Bucky turned and went back, careening out of the hallway and past the dislodged exterior door, calling out to Hobart for the tool. Twenty meters up the road the flamed-haired woman shouted into her mobile phone, mascara coursing down her chubby jowls. Bucky found the cutters—two young women had already taken refuge in the van—then, as he turned toward the house, a third girl ran out wailing. The edge of her blanket caught on a broken door hinge, tearing it from her shoulders as she bolted naked across the yard. On the rainy pavement she slipped and went down and slid halfway across, and Bucky took hold of her arm and jerked her upright and shoved her toward the open doors of the van.

As he reentered the house, Rolle stormed past him carrying a girl under each arm, hollering "Move! Move!" to clear a path, as more women of every age and skin tone dashed out from their cribs. He carried the bolt cutters to the bedroom where Sangita waited; she raised and tightened the chain and he cut it with a hard snap. In that moment their eyes met and he witnessed the impossible—like Durga with her arms flashing, Sangita came into her powers. In an instant she freed the bound girl from her chains and they scrambled into the hallway, rushing toward the street and the waiting van.

An altogether different sound came from the upper floor—a muffled baying that grew in volume and alarm. Wax listened intently as the sound became a panicked squeal, then he roared past, bellowing, "I won't see a dog abused!"

Bucky ran after him as he pounded up the curving staircase. In semidarkness Wax rushed down a narrow corridor toward the racket. He hurled his shoulder against a door at the end of the hallway, splitting the wooden panel and forcing the lock. Inside, a bug-eyed sod in a lime-green tracksuit stood with his pants around his ankles, pressing a King Charles spaniel against the side of a bed. To his left was the airline pet cage. Wax went for the man and stamped on his foot ferociously. At his howl of pain, a looping hook sprayed his teeth across the bed. Wax lifted the trembling dog and began to comfort her as he returned to the hallway.

A commotion broke out below them and on the stairs, and then the final battle began. Two men—a young Brit with the chest and arms of an iron pumper, and a mustached man with a cricket bat—tore into the upper corridor. Here was the help the fat madam had begged for. An endless second passed as they all sized up their chances, then Wax shouted, "Take her!" as he flipped the dog to Bucky and met his attackers.

The tight passage gave him one advantage: the younger man was so wide at the shoulders that the batsman couldn't get around him to strike a blow. But the iron pumper proved he could fight with all four limbs. He blocked Wax's jabs and uppercuts and came back with a Muay Thai chopping elbow and a vicious jumping knee strike. Jackie tried to kick the man's legs out from under him, but the move failed. He took a hard rabbit knee to the side of the head, and kept his footing only by clenching and grappling, as they gouged and bit and struggled for an opening to land a punch. Bucky's stomach turned as he saw that if Jackie went down, the thugs would hammer them both to death. Then Wax landed a brutal head butt and a slashing hand across the throat, dropping his foe to the floor. With rotten luck the man fell across his boots.

The smaller adversary saw the opening and drew back his cricket bat. "Pie thrower!" he snarled, taking a crabbed swing. Wax could only extend a massive hand to catch the blade. There was a sickening slap-crack of wood on flesh and breaking bones, but the bat stopped in mid-arc. In the next moment a final blow from Jackie's right fist blew apart the batsman's face.

"You got the spaniel, guv'nor?" he said calmly, as if nothing untoward had happened. "We had best withdraw before they get up more reinforcements."

FOURTEEN

The lesson of the Luton raid may have been that battles often hang in the balance, and only courage tips that balance to one side or the other. But in Bucky's mind, the take-away was that life sometimes requires a direct approach. Now he insisted that Yuri reveal the purpose of the closed meetings at the house, claiming a partner's right to know. After securing a pledge of secrecy and bolting the door behind them, Yuri began to speak, meandering from random factoids to a sting of irrelevant anecdotes. He explored the bleak territory of austerity and the moribund economy, the impotent government and lack of jobs, the soaring prices of commodities, the weakening pound and euro, the declining West and the rising Asian dragon.

Bucky saw that he was going round a children's pony circle. "Enough, just spit it out."

Yuri threw back the last of his vodka before coming clean. "Only a new currency will solve Britain's problems. When the palladion replaces the pound, a wealthier day will dawn."

Bucky laughed in his face. "There's no such thing as the palladion."

"Ah, but you are wrong, *tovarish*. Witness this!" From a cabinet Yuri withdrew a heavy leather bag like a medieval money pouch; he loosened the drawstring and poured out dozens of gleaming metal coins. Bucky took up one of the coins, turning it over, recognizing from the color and weight that the disk was pure palladium. The front bore a die-stamped image of the Clock Tower and the Eye, and above it the words "100 Palladion," while the edges were stamped with a repeated incuse: "Backed by Bullion." On the reverse side was a raised likeness of a peculiar man with a goatee.

"We have minted this small horde to showcase the artful design," Yuri said proudly, cradling the remaining coins in the money pouch as if he held a baby.

"Who's the dude on the back?"

"Is Russian patriot, Felix Dzerzhinsky. Nicolai Vasilievitch has always felt great admiration for Iron Felix."

"So Klepakov is behind this? And what's this crap about being backed by bullion? You can't think that people are going to carry around metal coins, instead of paper or plastic."

"Certainly not, our benefactor is no fool. But any currency that is convertible into bullion will always inspire greater trust, and Nicolai Vasilievitch stands ready to supply the Crown with the necessary palladium reserves, from his mines in Norilsk-Talnakh."

Bucky was certain that Yuri and the scheming oligarch were out of their skulls, but he played along, curious to know their plans. "Suppose the palladion did replace the pound, how would you work out the valuation and the exchange rates?"

Yuri was ready for this, and began to recite, "The worth of one palladion equals one one-hundredth of an ounce of palladium bullion. The exchange rate against the pound shall be one to ten."

"That would value the pound at less than half its present worth."

Yuri shrugged. "To victor belong spoils. Reverse is also true."

Ever since hearing his fractured analysis of the thousand -year cycles in British history, Bucky had suspected that their oligarch master was cooking up something truly monstrous. Now he knew what. But as he recalled the epic struggle that had been necessary to replace the European national currencies with the euro, he felt a surge of confidence—government ministers and financiers of every type and stripe would stand as one to defend the pound, and resist the introduction of any replacement. It occurred to him that many of those men were actually members of their club; they wouldn't need to look far for the downfall of Klepakov's ludicrous scheme.

"You'd have to persuade dozens of powerful men to go along with your plan, and I can't see any reason they would. They'd be acting against their own economic interests."

Yuri smiled inscrutably. "Naturally some men will have doubts, but we shall find the arguments to persuade them."

Again Bucky turned over the coin, noting the heft and the not-so-subtle messages conveyed by the design. "May I keep this one as a sample?"

Yuri snapped his fingers and held out an open palm. "Not yet, *tovarish*. But soon."

■ ■ ■

With Jackie Wax off work—a consequence of the plaster cast on his left hand—Bucky had taken on the role of temporary bartender. He was as bad a barman as any in London, or so his customers told him, but the company was worth the disgrace: the cocktail banter in the Grand Saloon could be almost as enlightening as the dialogues in Will Beard's cab. Within the club, certain men habitually avoided other members, and if they arrived with carnal intent, insisted on being shown directly to the bedrooms. But the pleasure drinkers were more gregarious, joking and blathering between stints at the craps or baccarat tables. Bucky was serving a banker and a barrister, hanging on their conversation while pretending to clean the glassware. He expected them to tout their latest scores, but the banker revealed how he had been suckered.

"It was a property syndication in the Algarve. The trout fly was guaranteed cash flow. Blocks of apartments, professional management, minimum investment of two hundred and fifty thousand pounds, and mind you, I put in double that sum. I was counting on three thousand pounds a month, all taxes deferred. Never imagined it could be a fraud. I'll tell you this, old man, smart crime pays smartly indeed."

"Have arrests been made?" the barrister asked, predictably.

"Pickpockets get prison time, white-collar criminals get a knighthood. The syndicators set up leasing companies within holding companies within foreign corporations. You can be certain they're insulated from personal consequences."

"Any idea who was behind it?"

"The Dzerzhinsky Group, or something along those lines."

Bucky bit his tongue until it bled. It was the first open mention he had heard of the oligarch's entity.

"Felonious bastards!" the barrister jeered, in lieu of commiseration. "By the way, speaking of gloom and doom, what do you see coming in the years ahead?"

The banker was on his third Navy rum, and the liquor seemed to fuel his rhetoric. "Absolute death and destruction, I'm afraid. The end of Western civilization. Scattered rioting and looting at first, then mass unrest. Troops brought in to put down the yobs, but in the end abandoning us to our fate. If we're lucky we'll be dragged into the streets and bludgeoned. The less fortunate will succumb to starvation."

"I'm reassured by your clairvoyance."

He enjoyed a last sweet swallow. "Naturally some will see it through pleasantly, just as they weathered the World Wars. Fortune rewards the prudent few."

Krassy and Sassy arrived to whisk the banker to their

playroom, and his outlook brightened. "Aha! My Bulgarian sprites! Have you missed me since our last tussle?"

Two days later an enigmatic new member known to Bucky only as "A. Smith" appeared in the Saloon. Oddly, Yuri had handled the enrollment, volunteering nothing about the man's background. It was the midday break—well before the evening influx—and Bucky assumed that the gray-suited "Smith" had come for a nooner with one of the girls; the man slipped into a leather armchair and salvaged a copy of the *Times* from an end table. As Bucky approached, he noticed that Smith had two unusual facial marks, prominent burns on his left cheek that resembled a dark-red mouse and mushroom. He asked if he could bring a drink.

"Whisky, neat." Then, after a pause, "Didn't expect to find an American working here."

When he returned with the liquor, the *Times* was folded to expose a story about trends in immigration. "The land of opportunity," Bucky said with faint humor.

Smith fixed him with a sterner expression. "Her Majesty's Government might take a somewhat different view. Given the current challenges, it's not in our interest to have jobs going to foreigners, permitted or otherwise." He put a sharp edge to the last part.

"I'm just filling in for our usual barman. But I do have a valid work permit."

"Yes, I'm sure you do." Smith looked away and flapped to the next page of his paper. He seemed ill at ease, and began to hum a nonsense melody between sips of Glenmorangie.

Something about the phrasing triggered Bucky's interest. "So are you in government?"

The drink nearly spilled. "Look here, that's no concern of yours so long as my bill is paid. And on the odd chance that we have any acquaintances in common, I really must insist that none of this ever come up in conversation, are we clear?"

Thankfully Amanda appeared at that moment and conducted Smith to the Classical Bedroom.

Later that week, in a coincidence that raised more questions than it answered, Beard telephoned with an invitation to a party at Westerley Park. Bucky had always sensed that the Brits had private channels of communication at every level of society—within their closed circles, decisions were taken that seemed inexplicable to outsiders. So was this his reward for embracing "accommodation" and enlisting in Sangita Sharma's crusade? He couldn't know. When asked about dress and arrangements for the evening, Beard had said only, "Jacket and tie, and I'll drive," but he turned up the following Saturday wearing what must have been his best suit, in place of his usual Donegal cap and frayed woolen car coat. His cab was freshly washed and shined.

Bucky smelled citrus air freshener as he got in. "What's up with all this?"

"It's a bit of a special occasion, but I won't spoil the surprise. Her Grace wants to make the announcement once the principal guests arrive."

They followed the same route to the estate as on Bucky's prior visit, but this time well after sunset, their passage carrying them from the illuminated monuments and edifices of central London to the darkness of rural Berkshire. The long driveway that transited the fields of Westerley Park was dimly defined by hanging candle lamps, but at the turn by the lake, which revealed a full view of the manor, the great house rose up before them, an incandescent blaze against the surrounding blackness. Two valets in red jackets and bow ties stood at the edge of the circular drive, near the base of the entry steps. In the area between the manor and the carriage house, dozens of cars were formed up in neat rows, the chauffeurs waiting idly, smoking and chatting, sizing up each other's vehicles. Reluctantly Beard handed off his keys to one of the valets, then they mounted the stairs and joined the guests inside the entry hall.

The Duchess spotted them at once and rushed over, calling out, "Wills, you're finally here! I have been beside myself with everything that needed doing!" She kissed him on the cheek and squeezed his arm.

"Not to worry, Your Grace, everything looks perfectly lovely."

"Mr. Newman, I trust you are enjoying your busy life in London?"

"Never a dull moment." He paused, ignoring the formalities until Beard reminded him with a fake cough. "—Your Grace."

"When you visited previously, it was just the three of us, but this evening you shall meet my many friends. I hope you find them stultifying."

"Stimulating, Your Grace," Beard interjected.

"I'm sure of it," Bucky put in. "If you don't mind, I'll wander around. It's an amazing property, I'd like to explore it again."

The Duchess swept her hand in a wide welcoming arc, as if to invite him to throw open every closet in the place, and he turned away toward the series of rooms that led to the Long Gallery. As he made his way through the salon, the library, and the dining room, he found himself seeing the property through more educated eyes, after experiencing the complete metamorphosis of the Belgrave Square house. This was a country that held up fine carpentry and cabinetmaking as a moral virtue, but the joinery and embellishments at Westerley Park couldn't match the product of Yuri's Polish and Russian crews. And for all its grandeur, the estate lacked the mythological elements that imparted such richness to the bordello's halls and bedrooms. The guests, on the other hand, were a noteworthy assortment of politicians and ministers, theater actors, bejeweled society types, titled gentry with their honorary medals and two or three senior military officers in dress uniform. Bucky quickly concluded that he was the youngest person at the party, apart from the waiters who glided from room to room with canapés and drinks. He wondered how he would get through the evening without speaking with other company, and worse, how he would explain himself if forced to engage.

He wandered aimlessly, turning away from anyone who posed a threat of conversation. In the Long Gallery he contemplated once again the portraits of kings and noblemen, and the crayon impression of the Duchess's late hubby. Near the far end of the gallery he thought he recognized a familiar figure, though initially he couldn't place the man; he moved a bit closer and simultaneously the head turned to show its profile. At once he saw the dark-red burn marks and recognized A. Smith. He reversed course and moved to flee the room, throwing a quick glance over his shoulder to see if he had been spotted. But Smith was also leaving the Long Gallery, by the exit at the opposite end.

Bucky turned back again, hoping he could somehow avoid a direct encounter through the remainder of the evening. A waiter passed with a tray of drinks, and he snagged two champagnes; he downed one in a gulp and began to nip at the other, while shuffling backward into a dark recess of the room. He tried to wish himself into invisibility, imagining the guests moving up and back along the walls of the gallery as schools of fish, perpetually circling some immense aquarium. Sharks, rays, cod, jacks, they all swam past, semi-aware of each other but not biting for the moment. When some time had passed, and his second champagne glass was nearly empty, the Duchess returned; she flashed a yellowed smile his way, and he went over to her with a question.

"You know the older gentleman, bald with two red marks on his face. Who is he?"

"That's Richard, one of my dearest Whitehall chums. He's Director General of UK Visas and Immigration. Would you like me to introduce you?"

"I wouldn't think of bothering him. Please forget I even asked." He moved away before the Duchess could respond, and she returned to her original purpose. From the center of the Long Gallery, she exhorted everyone to assemble in the salon for a musical performance.

On Bucky's first visit she had crowed about the period music at her parties; he wasn't entirely sure what kind of music that was, but as he followed the other guests into the salon, a weighty woman in concert black was taking her place at the Broadwood harpsichord. The Duchess offered a brief introduction, and the performer delivered a little talk about Bach's Partitas and English Suites, tossing out terms that sounded like *saraband* and *gigue* and *burlesca*. Then her plump fingers began to scamper over the keys, filling the room with the harmonious counterpoint of the Baroque.

Bucky stood at the back of the circle that gathered around the harpsichord, casting cautious glances for A. Smith as he pondered how long the musical interval might last. The pieces were complex, with melodies that he would never be able to whistle; feeling bored after just a few minutes, he began to wander again. He had seen the Duchess' vast collection of figurines on his prior visit, but now he noticed a display case on a table in a corner, containing a selection of round or rectangular porcelain boxes. Each little box was decorated with enamel portraits of pastoral scenes or ladies in eighteenth-century attire. The case had no label or explanatory cards; puzzled by the strange objects, he moved on, glad for the waiters who skirted the throng with more drinks. When the performance concluded, the guests began to flood out of the salon and into the adjoining rooms, but before he could follow, the harpsichordist came straight over to him. She was pissing drunk.

"Hiya sugar, have you seen the Carriage House? It's so much more private than this old barn. Let me show it to you, Tilly won't mind."

"Who?"

"The Duchess. I assumed you knew her name." She snaked an arm around Bucky's and tried to lead him from the room, but something told him to resist. He extricated his arm, saying, "I've never heard that kind of music played on a harpsichord. You've really got some chops."

"Thanks, you're an angel. Now listen, the concert's over, I'm desperately alone, and you're the only straight and single man at this party. Most of these sorry toffs couldn't get it up with a scaffold…but you look like you could manage. There's a room at the back of the Carriage House, and no one's going to miss us." She renewed her savage grip on his elbow.

Bucky remembered the strange collection of porcelain boxes. "I can see you know a lot about old music. Maybe you can tell me about these antique pieces in the corner?"

"Let's make it quick, lover," she prodded, as he moved toward the display case.

"So what the hell are these?"

She laughed gaily. "Those are patch boxes! Ladies of that era used leather beauty spots to cover their smallpox scars and syphilitic chancres. The boxes hold the patches and the glue used to apply them, along with blush and a little mirror under the lid."

Bucky was suddenly more determined to get away—he thanked the potted fugue player and made a forceful exit. He found the Duchess and Beard standing arm in arm near the fireplace in the library; beside them was a lanky man in a salmon jacket and paisley ascot, sporting a pair of round tortoiseshell glasses. His whiskers had been shaped to a pencil point, with the ends of his mustache greased and twisted into curlicue pigtails.

"Wills, did you enjoy Mr. Creacher's volume of verse about Edward VII?" the Duchess was saying to Beard. Bucky realized that the odd-looking gent was the poet whose work she had read aloud during his first visit to Westerley Park.

"It was certainly a great challenge to the mind. As the Bard might have put it, 'we need more light to find your meaning out.'"

Creacher smiled broadly as if he had received a compliment. "Speaking of Shakespeare, I acquired a remarkable insight into his works during my tour of American colleges, whilst I was giving public readings of my poetry."

The Duchess beamed. "Please tell us what you discovered, Philo."

"It seems that for centuries we have labored under a monumental delusion. I have it on the best authority from a critic in California that no one can 'understand' Shakespeare, nor interpret his work with any solid foundation. We had all foolishly thought that if you studied British history and culture and the roots of our language, you could eventually read Shakespeare with genuine comprehension. But it turns out that every text—whether *King Lear* or *King Kong*—is subject to an infinite range of interpretations, none any better or worse than the rest. Therefore, to the enlightened reader, all of English literature is meaningless."

"I've never heard such a thing!" Beard cried. "Shakespeare, Austen, and Dickens worthless, why it boggles the mind."

"I assure you it's quite true. I learned this at one of the best American schools."

"What a scintillating concept!" said the Duchess.

"Sniveling, Your Grace," Beard corrected.

Bucky approached the eccentric poet. "I don't know much about literature, but there's one thing that doesn't make sense. If your verse is meaningless, how do you structure and compose it?"

Creacher's eyes lit up. "Ah, but that's the liberating part. Realizing that I am doomed to render wretchedness has freed me from any fear of failure. Now I write without formal constraint, knowing that in sophisticated eyes, my work is the equal of the Bard's."

The Duchess frowned at her empty whisky. "Wills, would you be a dear and get me another single malt? I asked a waiter ages ago. It was obviously a feudal gesture."

Beard seemed troubled by her request for more sauce. "May I splash a bit of water in the glass, or at least some ice?"

"Certainly not! No one shall accuse me of being self-diluted."

He went off and quickly returned with another double, then pulled Bucky aside. "Here's the long and the short of it. Her Grace intends to announce our engagement this evening, but she wants to wait until the royals have arrived. They were due hours ago. I told her just get on with it, but she doesn't want to give up on a higher audience."

Bucky's eyes bulged. "Do you mean to say—"

"Down a notch from the Sovereign. But still the bluest blood."

In her agitation the Duchess had blasted her drink, and now began to teeter. Beard moved discreetly to take her arm, an apparent gesture of affection that had the advantage of preventing her from toppling over. He stole a glance at his watch, then looked to Bucky with concern. Finally, just at the moment of despair, a protective officer in thick-soled shoes entered the library, holding open the door for his charges.

"My dear friends," the Duchess sang out, "it is a great honor and privilege to welcome to Westerley Park Their Royal Highnesses the Prince of Wiles and the Duchess of Cornmeal."

FIFTEEN

Each month Zhanna Dolgorukov dispatched new and ever-more-urgent pleas, calling out for rescue from the tedium of Krasnogorsk. Now the three boys added their voices, declaring their affection for their father, protesting his long absence, prodding him to find them work in Britain as bricklayers, framers, or painters. Suddenly feeling as well as looking his age, Yuri saw the only path to solace. He would bring his wife and sons to London without further delay.

He found Bucky in the house kitchen, breakfasting on an expired yogurt after his evening at Westerley Park. "I have spoken with Nicolai Vasilievitch. Our grand guardian promises to secure four work visas, in exchange for equitable modification of terms."

"What modification?"

"Trivial adjustment in his share of proceeds, to sixty-six point six percent of future revenues. It is nothing compared to the love of one's family, do you not agree?"

Bucky wanted to smash his coffee mug on the tile and shout, *Pay the bastard with your own money!* But the invocation of Yuri's flesh and blood stopped him cold. He fell back on badgering his partner. "I happen to know the man in charge of UK Visas and Immigration. He told me that Whitehall takes a dim view of more jobs going to foreigners, permitted or otherwise. You're gonna have more trouble than you think."

"But this is selfsame man who will assist me! Nicolai Vasilievitch assures me of Director General's cooperation."

"Why would he lift a finger for you?"

"We speak of new member who calls for Amanda, yes? Faced with film of their passion, how can he refuse his help?"

Bucky's jaw dropped open in a cartoon expression. "You have a video of them in bed?"

"*Da, tovarish.* At our splendid benefactor's direction, every liaison in this house is filmed. Hidden cameras in each bedroom feed to master disk. Is simple system—after seven days, change disk. Easy to duplicate most energetic scenes, for purposes of persuasion."

Bucky staggered away, his knees wobbling and his head spinning wildly toward nausea. Half awake, he tried to grasp the implications of what Yuri had so casually revealed. Then at last he understood. The club had been nothing but a scheme for shame on an industrial scale. Scores of MPs and government figures, corporate chieftains and financiers, titled lords and elevated sods who gripped the levers of power had been captured by the house cameras. This had nothing to do with private blackmail or family favors—the circle who could have defended the pound against the palladion were now the oligarch's *suki.*

When he'd first learned of the currency scheme, he assumed it was just a ploy to flog palladium bullion to the Crown. Russia was the sole source, and Klepakov controlled the mines. It couldn't have been simpler. But looking back on his years in Manhattan, he felt the pieces of a giant jigsaw puzzle snap together with terrible force. He had arrived in New York soon after the financial crisis, with the investment houses still burning and the road-killed corpses of derivatives hustlers clogging every gutter. He had marked the hollow eyes of bankrupted men as they staggered from Nassau to Broad Street, and watched them linger too long on the benches at Battery Park. Like the margin traders of the '29 crash, they had bet the wrong side of a phony boom, and years of depression lay ahead. But craftier men had refused to be suckered. They'd smelled the coming carnage and gobbled up out-of-the-money puts for pennies on the dollar. When the tower of stinking paper collapsed, they cashed out their options for billions. *Here* was the oligarch's real game. Like Soros in the nineties, like the plotting put-buyers of September '08, Klepakov would massively short the pound and then engineer its destruction.

Suddenly the wheels were coming off and he was tumbling out of control. Through the initial remodeling and staffing up, and the months of euphoria and turmoil that followed, he had always assumed that Yuri was his friend. He had never acknowledged the debt that he owed—and Yuri had never begrudged it. But he knew that without the buoy and line that had been thrown his way that first night in the pub in Tottenham, he would have slipped beneath the surface. As their journey began he had feared every kind of crass exploitation, but his savvy, talented comrade had defied all the stereotypes—and, more importantly, had treated him as a brother, whether celebrating victory or wracked by loss. Now he questioned whether he had been duped. Yuri must have known from the start that the club's members would be secretly filmed, but had said nothing, playing him for a fool. It wasn't the sort of thing a friend would do.

Robotically he washed and dressed and forced himself into his normal routine, hoping it would rein in the madness. Instead he found himself turning over the past decade of his life, searching for the point of error. In the years after college, as he made a name for himself and then took to rooming with Dayna, he had been certain that he was marching down the proven path. Hadn't everyone agreed, *This is how it's supposed to go?* You live together until you're certain it's love, buy your honey a ring and a lavish wedding, then it's two-point-two kids and a house in the burbs for the next quarter-century. Sure, the mattress matadors talked about camping out in Manhattan forever, girl-of-the-month and no entanglements. But he had always known where that ended—bachelorhood and rehab at forty. At its core, he found nothing to be wished for in the formulaic life. Now all of it was vanishing before his eyes: work, values, self-respect, any chance at love, and he was flailing helplessly in a nest of snakes, perversely tangled with sex and money, power and politics, the dull requirements of day-to-day business and the hypocrisies of his secret war. He had awoken feeling satisfied with the balance he had struck, playing off his ongoing work at the club against his hacker pranks and raids on other sex-sellers. But whatever peace of mind he had known had just been obliterated.

He sensed that the root of his troubles lay in his own identity, and his inability to understand who and what he had become. On his first day in London, when Will Beard tossed out the tale of the Newmanry, he had found it tempting to tell himself, *That's me!* A hero of technology—even more, a shaper of history—and the perfect model for a triumphal self-image. But he had taken the stage in different costume for his role at International Fulfillment. It wasn't precisely a villain's part, but the back-office boss of a Belgrave Square bordello wouldn't pass for a war hero. And his confusion had grown a hundredfold when Sangita Sharma threw down her moral gauntlet before the statue of John Henry Cardinal Newman. Somewhere within it all was the answer he was seeking, but he still couldn't balance the equation of the two Newmans, or find a way to combine and resolve their attributes. That left him unsure of anything in his life.

As the morning grew blacker he gave in to the impulse to contact Sangita and confess what he had learned. As much as anyone, she was entitled to know the oligarch's plans. He sent a text, asking for a meeting. She responded that she planned to come into central London later in the afternoon, and asked him to wait for her in Parliament Square. When she arrived, they sat on the stone ledge in the shadows of the western side, gazing across at the great hunched back of the Churchill statue. The majestic structures commanding their view filled him with empty sadness; it was the same barren nothingness he had suffered when he lost his job. He had not been face-to-face with Sangita since the Luton raid, and she seemed different somehow. He detected no physical change, but her presence carried him back to the slave house. Amid the chaos she had become the goddess, and he wondered how this unassuming woman could possibly wield such power, while he felt utterly powerless.

He told her everything about the palladion plot, the *suki* and the secret video system. And for the first time, he shared with her the identities of the men atop their member's list—International Fulfillment's most illustrious punters. Repeatedly she drew in her breath at the shock of a household name.

"This is a threat to the nation. I cannot stand by silently, regardless of any danger to my mother or myself. I will take this to the police."

"You'd be wasting your time. The only way to stop Klepakov is to bring him all the way down. A prison term, deportation, something final or fatal. It's not going to happen. He can blackmail the very same people who would have to move against him."

Sangita leaped to her feet, wheeling to confront him. "You chose to eat from the crocodile's table. Now will you do nothing as the beast devours us all? I understand that you are American. Perhaps you think this is not your fight. You're wrong—your life and soul are at stake. Please, if you have a conscience, wake up and do what is right."

And there it was, stark and pressing, the choice that he had avoided and feared. He let himself fall against the stone until he lay on his back, staring into the sky. He found no solution there. Through the prior weeks, as he jerked the rug from under the predators that Devi Way opposed, ruining their businesses and maddening the operators, he had dug a deep moat around his own vocation. He'd told himself the Belgrave Square house stood above and apart from the street crime and the slave dens, far better on its face, and morally excused in light of his work to topple the real offenders. That rationale was dead.

"I came here to deploy trading apps for a securities firm in the City. Two weeks later I'm helping a Russian oligarch launch a brothel in Belgravia. I lost the girl I planned to marry. On the rebound I fell for a dominatrix. Now all I have is a Swiss bank account and a secret life waging war on scumbag pimps. I don't know who I am or what I am or what the hell I'm supposed to do with my time on this planet."

Sangita dragged him to his feet by his coat sleeve. "You have been seduced by a false idea—the ugly lie that the world consists only of ones and zeros, predators and prey. Please come with me into the Abbey. I will show you a better way to look at life."

Bucky had never entered Westminster Abbey, considering it just another in a series of less-than-Catholic churches. And he had no patience for any religious appeal. "You know that I haven't been to Mass in years. I don't believe in the supernatural," he protested.

Sangita tightened her grip on his arm. "What I want to show you is entirely of this world. Come with me now."

He allowed her to lead him across Broad Sanctuary and through the Great North Door. The interior was still and ancient and lighted only by weightless beams that filtered through the pastel windows; an organist was practicing, and seismic pedal notes vibrated through the interior space. At a distance, an Anglican father in a brown cassock conversed with an elderly woman.

Sangita guided Bucky past the six chapels of the northern transept and nave, and the Henry VII Lady Chapel; then, beyond the sacrarium, she turned into Poet's Corner. "Chaucer, Dickens, Dryden, Johnson, think of the intelligences buried here," she whispered. They moved among the jumbled grave markers and the newer memorial stones, reading the names and dates, marking the occasional quote as epitaph. Near the center lay a square black slab, more recently laid down. "See the memorial stone for George Eliot? She was a favorite of mine, in school. The bordering inscription is from her first book. 'The first condition of human goodness is something to love; the second something to reverence.'"

Bucky was silent, considering the words until Sangita spoke again. "I have always known that what I most revere is simple justice. As for love, I continue to hope. Do you believe in human goodness? Do you want to be a good man? You could join me in the charity. We could accomplish good works together."

"And quit International Fulfillment?"

"It is your choice. But I ask you, what do you love, and what do you revere? The rest of your life will flow from the answers to these questions."

SIXTEEN

K lepakov's clandestine meetings—organized to bolster support for the palladion—now came at closer intervals, and with spears to their spines, the *suki* grimly attended. As the co-opted Brits took their places at the table, the cheers and back-slapping ended, and only the clamor of outraged protests rang from the Salon. Bucky noted the faces and titles in the expanding circle of worthies: the MPs chairing the Treasury Committee and the Public Accounts Committee; high officers of principal British banks; a media baron fond of shaping public opinion; the Deputy Chancellor of the Exchequer. Their dour expressions hinted at how the oligarch had made them his collaborators. For the bulk of the ambushed *suki*, the words "We have you on video" had proved sufficient. But Yuri revealed how one stubborn MP had been forced to attend a private screening of his turn at bouncing Isabelle, while a senior minister and a securities exec only caved after being confronted with striking blow-ups of their threesome with Kimiko.

Bucky had assumed that anything so momentous as the adoption of a new national currency would require endless public debate and Parliamentary table-pounding. But like most things that mattered in the new millennium, the cut-over to the palladion era was being handled the old-fashioned way: with cynical trade-offs and arm-twisting in smoke-filled rooms. One CEO of a City-based bank decided to dig in his heels, daring Klepakov, "Go ahead and tell my wife, she knows perfectly well that I enjoy the odd mistress." But when he was handed a DVD compilation of his erotic exploits, inside an envelope addressed to a rising rival at his bank, he thought better of his defiance.

According to Yuri, the oligarch had already boosted the bullion shipments from his mines. From this expanded supply, a larger horde of palladion coins would be privately minted—free samples for key supporters. A marketing campaign was brewing, too; that was how Bucky interpreted the piles of shrink-wrapped four-color documents stacked in the corners of the Salon. Fact sheets and white papers in seven languages touted the benefits of the new currency, their claims heavily buttressed by charts and graphs and analysis put forward by "leading economists." Oddly, not a word about these plans had appeared in any newspaper, nor had any online portal or even a private blog revealed the secret. The momentum toward some sort of grand introduction reminded him of the final days before International Fulfillment put out its gleaming door plaque, but this would be the opposite of the club's understated opening. When Klepakov went public about the palladion, all the world would know.

Even as these grandiose plans advanced, Bucky's focus was fixed on the smallest of things. Tiny lenses and telltale wires had become his obsession. He tossed the bedrooms whenever Yuri left the house—he flipped heavy mattresses, disassembled lamps and sconces, scrutinized the corners of the crown molding and the dusty recesses of the coffered ceilings. He aimed his flashlight into air return vents and turned back the folds of brocaded curtains. He inspected mounted decorations, examined gilded picture frames, and opened up every cabinet and armoire. But he couldn't find the hidden cameras.

The cover-up enraged him; even the digital recording system was hidden away in some closet that he couldn't locate. He longed to view the shameful footage that had cowed the *suki*. But Yuri had employed his considerable skills to safeguard the precious files.

He was drinking in the Grand Saloon, killing time and tension, when Natalie entered, fresh from a session. He thought he had seen all of her spanking costumes—the suggestive apparel she wore to titillate her clients—but she had a new ensemble, a mock corporate look with a glossy white PVC blouse and a pencil skirt in butter-soft black leather. Navy pumps completed the outfit. When she turned to take a seat at a table near the bar, he realized that the skirt was bottomless. He offered to mix a cocktail. She waved it off and he flopped into a chair across the table.

"So do you have those web tactics for me?"

He had completely forgotten his promise. "I'm still thinking. I'll have something for you soon."

She saw through him at once, and flashed a look that let him know it. "Well at least I've been busy. My videos are going gangbusters. I need more, and soon, but Angelica has come to my rescue. Last Saturday she took me to a fetish club in Brixton—"

"You mean Cruel Britannia?" Bucky interrupted, suddenly alert.

"Don't tell me you've been there? Then you know the stage at the front of the disco. Angelica dragged me up there…we were both in costume, she has this darling Nazi outfit, and I went as a skoolgurl. We improvised a little scene of discipline and domination, and the place went wild. Then I realized, people would pay loads of money if we filmed our play and sold it on KnottyNatalie.net."

He tried to picture Angelica and Natalie together—it was almost too hot to imagine. "Has she agreed to appear with you in fetish films?"

"More than agreed, we're cooking up two new scripts. We start shooting next week, the working titles are *Bound and Determined* and *Margaret Thrasher*."

The political allusion reminded him of the hidden cameras. Hoping to give nothing away, he inquired which room she used for her sessions with Klepakov. She told him that the oligarch always insisted on the same small fifth-floor bedroom. "It's the one with no music. How's that for symbolism?"

Bucky was puzzled; he thought that Yuri had wired every room in the house for sound. Then it hit him. *What if the speakers were more than speakers?* A part of him wanted to jump up from the table and tear apart the household audio system, but he forced himself to wait, pretending what Natalie had revealed was of no consequence. He shifted topics again, asking about her research. "You told me once that you're studying neurology. Do you know much about the brain?"

She stared at him incredulously. "I've done graduate work in neuroanatomy and histochemistry, and dissected more human and animal brains than you've had hot meals. What is it you want to know?"

His face reddened, but he plowed ahead. "I know a man who's a kind of street genius. Whatever you bring up, he has every fact and figure on the tip of his tongue. He told me that his brain expanded while he was memorizing something called the Knowledge. Is that possible? Is it the size of our brains that matters most?"

"I assume your friend is a taxi driver? Whether cobbler or composer, true genius requires the integration of the two hemispheres of the brain, through the corpus callosum. Loads of people are brilliant at one thing, like music or languages, but if you want to understand da Vinci or Einstein, the secret is they got their right and left brains to work together synchronously. It's not easy, the hemispheres are natural opposites in some ways."

"Like dommes and subs?"

"Ha-ha, how adroit you are," she said without humor. Then, as Angelica appeared at the top of the staircase, she called out happily, "Speak of the devil!"

As Bucky turned, a changed woman glided into the Saloon. In every movement and expression the hard-cut angles and edges that defined Angelica Smuts had visibly softened. Even her inner ferocity—still crouching in the African grass—appeared to have been moderated into a firm contentment. In the months after his own failed attempts to befriend her, Bucky had asked himself what kind of man could satisfy Angelica, or if she wanted only a bound-and-flogged sort of fellow. Now, as she pulled out a chair by Natalie's side, he had his answer.

She flicked the sleeve of Natalie's blouse with her riding crop—"Smart top for a smart bottom"—then eased into the seat and smoothed her hand over the black leather skirt. "I wish I had a cat-o-nine tails in this hide, it's so soft we could play all night and never leave a mark. Would you enjoy that, *liefling*?"

Bucky cut in. "Natalie was telling me what it takes to be a genius. You need to persuade the opposite sides of your brain to play together nicely."

Angelica ignored him completely, drawing closer to Natalie and continuing to pet her. "Did you find that outfit in a shop or online?"

"Half and half. I got the top on the Internet and the skirt at a place in Soho. Have you seen the back? There isn't any!" She stood up and pirouetted, exposing her bare behind.

Angelica sucked in her breath in comic outrage. "Why, you wanton girl! If you don't behave yourself, Mommy's going to be *very* strict with you."

"Promises, promises." Natalie pushed out the pink tip of her tongue.

Angelica sprang from her chair with feline grace. "Come with me, young lady," she purred, drawing her along. As they moved toward the staircase, she urged the bottomless Natalie forward with playful little smacks of her crop. With each stroke, the blonde ponytail bounced.

▪ ▪ ▪

In the first bedroom that Bucky inspected, two in-wall speakers had been mounted at the narrow end, bracketing the window and facing the bed. Each of the speakers was head-high and was disguised by a grill cloth dyed to match the wall paint. Near the bottom of the grill was a small plastic logo with a crown emblem and the manufacturer's name. He peered carefully at both the left and right speakers; an almost imperceptible hole had been drilled through one of the logos. He removed the cloth cover, exposing a pinhole camera. A wire feed ran back into the wall. The next bedroom was fitted with the same setup, as was the one beyond—but on the fifth floor, at the end of the hallway, he found a small bedroom with no speakers, and no hidden camera. Here Natalie entertained the oligarch.

He had no background in surveillance, and his next steps carried him into unknown territory. He discovered that he could order a battery-powered wireless camera with a built-in microphone, which transmitted digital audio and video to a remote receiver. At that end, the file could be saved to any device of his choice. He considered the layout of the secluded bedroom, imagining where he might hide a camera and picturing the field of view that would result from various placements. A wireless camera hugely expanded the possibilities for concealment. When the gadget arrived, he slipped it into a spray of dried seed pods and flowering branches, in a vase on a corner table. The browns and umbers of the dried plants perfectly camouflaged the little device. The wide-angle lens wouldn't miss a thing that went on in the room.

He ran a test, propping up a magazine on the bed. The feed to the receiver in his office was remarkably clear—the portrait on the cover was easily recognizable; even the color palette was accurate. When all was ready, he spoke to Natalie again. "I've got an idea to help drive traffic to your site. But you need to trust me."

"I let people tie me up and discipline me. Trust isn't a problem."

Bucky gathered his courage and tried to sound relaxed. "The next time you're with Klepakov, when things get hot and heavy, just look toward the outside wall and smile."

"That's it?"

"Two more things. I need your ID and password for your web server. And later this month, you might need to join me on a road trip."

"Agreed, but if we're going to travel, Angelica will be coming along."

Over the following week, Bucky began recording Klepakov's sessions with Natalie. For once a gizmo worked as advertised: the compact wireless camera delivered digital magic. Hours of furious footage captured the oligarch in rolled-up shirtsleeves, his ruddy face beading with sweat as he bound and smacked and lustily thrashed his indifferent British partner. And the resolution was dazzling, allowing close-ups and special effects when the raw footage was edited. In a movie-making app, Bucky lovingly assembled his first real fetish film, combining scenes that he carefully joined with fades and soft transitions. In exquisite slow motion, the crop and cane rebounded off Natalie's battle-hardened bottom, while tight shots revealed the pervy delight in Klepakov's reptilian eyes. At the climax the handcuffed Natalie, adorable in a raised plaid skirt, looked up from over the oligarch's knee and flashed a brilliant smile and wink.

Bucky thought he had proved himself a gifted cinematographer, but he had to admit that the audio was rubbish. It wasn't a technical problem—the clarity was superb—rather, the steady *whap, snap* became mind-numbing, and he had recorded no dialogue to advance the limited plot. The clip needed a soundtrack. He tried overlaying some head-banging metal with a menacing beat, but it seemed contrived. Then he remembered Yuri's love of the Russian composers. Through a long afternoon he experimented with ballet scores and symphonic movements as accompaniment for his fetish flick. The effect was preposterous. Finally, searching online for Russian vocal music, he discovered *Boris Godunov*. He added the czar's brooding soliloquy, with English captions at the bottom of the frame. "I have attained the highest power...but my tortured soul knows no peace; in vain the fortune-tellers promised me a long and peaceful reign." He finished the file with bold titles offering the oligarch's full name and the URL of Natalie's new website. The edited clip ran just over two minutes, a perfect length for the web placement that he intended.

But an unexpected encounter would alter his plans. The change—he reflected much later—was a bit like adding a modest lump of uranium to an ordinary bomb. As he reentered Belgrave Square from a solitary afternoon walk through Hyde Park, he realized that he was being followed. He cut away hard to his right and went the wrong way around, pausing at the corners to flush the tail; when he was certain, he turned and confronted a somber, iron-haired man. He didn't recognize the face until they stood at arm's length. Here was the German diplomat who had taken Angelica's cheeky salute from an upper window of the embassy.

"Do not be alarmed, I wish only to ask a favor. I am Dietrich, the commercial attaché."

"You could have knocked at the door."

"Perhaps, but let us not quibble over details. As the continent's leading bankers, we are naturally concerned about the implications of a rival currency to the euro. We have been excluded from the many planning sessions conducted on your premises, and have not been invited to the introductory conference for the palladion. Could you perhaps secure two passes, for myself and a representative of the Deutsche Bundesbank?"

Bucky had no idea what Dietrich was talking about. "Which conference do you mean, exactly?"

"There is no need to be coy, Herr Newman! We know of your technical work in the securities industry. It is obvious that you are deeply involved in the effort to dump the pound. But since you require me to be specific, I speak of the private function at Cliveden, next Saturday evening."

Bucky bluffed. "No promises, but I'll see what I can do."

"*Danke für Ihre Bemühungen*. And since our brief dialogue has been frank and productive, I will advance one more request, of a delicate nature. Our ambassador would be personally grateful if no employee of your gentleman's club—even a beautiful woman—would ever again walk the streets of London in the uniform of the *Waffen SS*."

When Bucky brought up the website for Cliveden, four hundred years of British history leaped to life. The palatial estate north of Windsor had seen a duel between the Duke of Buckingham and the Earl of Shrewsbury, and the intrigues and ambitions of the Prince of Wales, the architect Charles Barry, and even Lord Astor. But all of it fell away before the scandal of the century—in a swimming pool added in the early sixties, loose and lovely Christine Keeler had met the Secretary for War, John Profumo.

"I want to attend the Cliveden conference," he told Yuri, later that evening.

His partner seemed appalled by the leak. "It is not your

place, *tovarish*. Only men of influence will attend. I urge you to forget whatever you have heard."

Bucky broke into a tap dance. "I'm just thinking about the practical arrangements. Klepakov doesn't speak English, unless you count 'fucking geek.' He could never make a persuasive speech. Maybe I can be useful…help you get your message across."

"Is constructive suggestion, but our video presentation has been scripted most artfully, and filmed by professional crew. Nicolai Vasilievitch will not need to speak."

"You made a promo film about the palladion?"

"Do we not live in age of media?"

Bucky turned away, leaving Yuri with the impression that he had given up. But in that moment he knew how Klepakov would come to grief.

That evening he slipped off to Piccadilly and bought a handful of prepaid cell phones; the following morning he placed a call from one of the burner phones to Meeting Services at Cliveden. Posing as a coordinator for the Dzerzhinsky Group, he expressed his concern that audiovisual support for the Saturday event might not be up to snuff. "I cannot stress too strongly the importance of video presentation." He moved his voice down into his chest, delivering his best imitation of Yuri's Moscow accent.

"I assure you, Mr. Borodin, our facilities are state-of-the-art, and our support personnel are of the highest caliber."

"Who isss your veedeo man," Bucky rumbled, laying on the accent. "I veesh to know his name."

"Just let me check. All right, I see that Crispin Pollock will be on duty Saturday evening."

Minutes into an online search, Bucky realized that he was looking at himself, at twenty. Each of young Pollock's social pages linked to his personal website—a mad mash-up of tech and media feeds and pix of his water-cooled gaming computer, with a further link to his strident blog. In the most recent posting, he rambled bitterly about "indiscriminate cloudmania," then evangelized the manifold advantages of Linux over UNIX. Bucky scanned the archive, clicking back through a dozen items. No one had ever commented on any of Pollock's rants.

That would change. *Finally, a media professional who understands the issues we face! Crispin Pollock is a brilliant voice crying in the wilderness, and one that should be recognized as a postmodern oracle.* Bucky used the handle Tor&More for his post.

Pollock quickly responded to the comment. He overflowed with gratitude and begged to know all about Tor&More.

Bucky did not answer. He waited a full day, amused by Pollock's frenzied queries. Then he sent an e-mail from Tor&More to the contact address listed on the personal website. *I'd like to pick your brains about IT and media trends, from a corporate perspective. Drinks are on me in central London, if you have the time(?)*

When Crispin Pollock arrived at the Wolf & Waif, Bucky realized why none of his sites had included a head shot. Flaxen hair jutted in tufts from his oblong potholed skull, and his ravaged skin had erupted in a rash of scabrous pimples. From across the table, his unbrushed teeth threw off a withering pong. He launched into a monologue about 5G infrastructure, coding languages, mobile apps, online games, media development, and British beer. Bucky nodded and smiled and bought round after round, which the younger man downed in eager gulps. Only when the torrent slowed did he attempt to steer the conversation.

"So what's your take on guerilla marketing? We think it could be important in our business."

Pollock appeared momentarily stumped, then finally

thought to ask question number one. "What business is that?"

Bucky grinned. "It's multifaceted, like anything else that works. There's a labor component, a services component, and we have facilities to look after. You know how it is."

"It sounds just like us."

"I'm sure it is." He motioned to the bartender for yet another round. "And all of us must be creative in getting our messages out. By the way, do you know what a full body massage is?"

Pollock scowled as if he had heard something idiotic. "I should think it is a massage of one's full body."

"That's the mistake most men make. Actually, what it means is, the girl uses *her full body* to massage *your full body*. Your *very* full body, if you see what I'm getting at."

Pollock did. More beer arrived and Bucky elaborated. "But I have always believed that's just the appetizer. For the entree, I like a team approach. Imagine a smashing blonde pressing her breasts to your face, while down below a hot brunette proves what mouths and tongues are meant for. Then get that massage girl going on your bum." He smiled knowingly.

"You're not saying you've actually experienced such things?" Pollock shifted awkwardly as if there were a problem with his pants.

"What I'm saying is, how would *you* like to experience it, this coming Saturday?"

"Oh Jesus please tell me you're not joking."

Bucky slipped a thumb drive and a business card from his pocket and placed them on the table. "Our guerilla marketing strategy requires us to play that video at the Dzerzhinsky Group meeting, on Saturday evening. Use it in place of the file you'll be given. As soon as our clip begins to run, leave Cliveden and come directly to the address on the card. Kandy, Ruta, and Chloe will be waiting for you. Feel free to spend the night with them, as our guest."

"I would lose my job if I did that! And wouldn't the police arrest me?"

"Believe me, Scotland Yard has more pressing matters. As far as your job goes, how much do you take home after taxes?"

"Nearly three hundred and thirty-two quid each fortnight," Pollock said proudly.

"You'll find an envelope with your name on it, in the bedroom where you'll spend Saturday night. Inside will be six months' wages."

At week's end, after putting off the moment as long as possible, Bucky resigned from International Fulfillment. His first inclination had been to recite the list of his contributions to the club and hold out his hand for equity. Abandoning that—out of a growing awareness of the storm that was coming—he worked up a sappy pitch for friendship, coupled with his hope to meet Yuri's wife and sons, soon to arrive in London. His final version was simpler: it was time to move on. Once settled, he would e-mail a forwarding address.

Yuri's face fell. "You are unhappy, *tovarish*? I do not wish to lose your many talents. Tell me what can be done."

"You know how people come and go. This isn't my permanent job."

"We have done famous work. No one in London has equaled our achievements."

"Fame can be a two-edged sword. Especially great fame."

Yuri's eyes filled with pain and he struggled for words, launching new appeals and then abandoning them mid-sentence, searching for the means to persuade his partner to reconsider. At last giving in, he shrugged and embraced Bucky in one of his soulful bear hugs—thankfully not kissing him.

■ ■ ■

The Great Hall at Cliveden had been designed with multitudes in mind, but its full expanse was strained by the roiling crush of men. Bankers, traders, financiers, and market makers; ministers, power brokers, and key parliamentarians; even, for the first time, print reporters and media flacks, had come together, some in the know, some drawn by whispers, for the public unveiling of a covert plan. The richly paneled hall had been cleared of furniture and decorated with both fixed and moving embellishments. Giant foil balloons in the shape of palladion coins floated overhead, tugging at their strings, and Krassy and Sassy—in gilded catsuits—circulated with serving trays, offering miniature money bags stuffed with real palladions. At the edge of the crowd stood Dietrich and another German, uninvited but holding proper papers. Overnight an envelope containing the required passes had been pushed through the mail slot on the embassy's door. Klepakov held court to the right of the dais, surrounded by his cronies; from the shoulders up, his confident visage might have been the bust of a czar. Only his brown cigarette undermined the image, as the oligarch flouted the smoking ban with a series of stinking puffs. A huge flat-screen monitor had been mounted high up on the wall—the display would be clearly visible even from the back of the chamber. A microphone on a metal stand stood directly below the screen.

When all was ready, the oligarch's English-speaking mouthpiece called for quiet. He thanked the mob for its attendance, damned Whitehall for imposing austerity, warned that only radical action would avert a calamity, and praised the eminent N. V. Klepakov for opening the road to recovery. "I ask you all to direct your full attention to the screen above me," he intoned, while nodding to a young man with an oddly shaped head and a ravaged complexion, visible behind a glass pane at the side of the room. The lights dimmed and moments later

Bucky's video began to play. Simultaneously, Crispin Pollock's spotty face vanished from behind the pane.

In the first unwary moments, as they watched the oligarch binding a lovely, half-naked English girl, many in the hall assumed they were viewing a humorous prologue—perhaps a risqué skit that lampooned the shackled British economy? But as the crops and canes came out and the real naughtiness began, a different sort of murmur rose from the crowd. The music swelled and the opera fans made the obvious connection, and the snorts and hoots of "Huh!" and "God!" suddenly changed to cackles. Then from the back of the room came a wild laugh, piercing and mad with glee, and as the hilarity spread, Klepakov shouted, *"Nyet! Stop!"* and made for the microphone stand. He raised it above his head and began to flail at the wall, desperate to smash the offending screen, but the pole was too short and he only dented the fine wooden paneling. Behind him a Palladion balloon came loose and popped against the ceiling. High above, to his horror, Natalie lay across his knee, her plaid skirt pulled up for a smacking. Klepakov's on-screen eyes watered with depravity, and the *suki* roared as they saw their blackmailer hoist by his own petard.

The racket only grew as Natalie winked and smiled into the camera, then changed to mocking peals as Klepakov lumbered to his feet, stuffed a hand down his baggy pants and rearranged his genitals. The reporters had their phones out, capturing the video. As the clip ended they forwarded the file to their editors. To the side, Dietrich was shouting into his mobile phone… insisting that he must speak at once with *der Kanzler.*

Across the room a hundred voices cried out, "Play it again, again!" But Bucky's directorial debut had concluded. Only a bold URL remained, static on the screen:

www.KnottyNatalie.net

Even as a famous new scandal exploded at Cliveden, a series of carefully scripted actions went forward elsewhere. Accompanied by Natalie, Angelica, Sangita, and her mother, Bucky left London Euston on an express train to Scotland. At Port Glasgow a seaworthy boat—chartered with a promise of absolute discretion—waited to whisk them from the harbor and deliver them to a cottage in the Hebrides.

Pulling out of the station, Bucky promoted the Klepakov film clip to Natalie's home page, then sent two texts. The first, to Yuri, read, *Leave now! Tell no one where you're going.* The second message, dispatched from yet another burner cell phone, was blasted out to a bulk list of network and cable news providers, wire services, and tabloids. It contained only the words *Oligarch Fetish Video*, and the address of Natalie's website.

"How long will we need to hide out?" Sangita asked, when Bucky revealed what he had set in motion.

He thought for a moment. "Either a few days, or the rest of our lives."

Later, north of Wigan, students near the front of the carriage sent up a gale of laughter. Bucky left his seat and ambled toward them, hoping to eavesdrop. They crowded around a tattooed boy in a tasseled cap, who held up his phone as it played an online video. Even from the phone's compact speaker, the strains of *Boris Godunov* were unmistakable.

One of the girls shrieked, "Look how that old pervert smacks her, and look at her smile! It's hilarious, post it to Facebook and YouTube."

Bucky returned to his seat, his heart banging.

"What was it?" Sangita asked.

"My video's gone viral."

▪ ▪ ▪

Two days later, sleepy-eyed and drained by travel, they stumbled from an ancient cottage into a misting fairy seascape. A cold clear sea lapped at the sand, the beach extending half around a hidden cove. Behind the stone cottage, the hills rolled up into emerald grasslands, as puffins soared from the rock cliffs at the northern edge of the cove.

"I'll make nashta and tea," Mukta Sharma said, covering a yawn. She had been sick on the tossing boat ride from Port Glasgow, as night obscured the horizon and set them spinning inside a darkened sphere. Sangita held her mother's head through the difficult day at sea that followed, as Bucky reassured Mukta that their voyage would end as fortuitously as her first, from Mumbai to Liverpool. When at last they put ashore, late in the evening, Bucky and his four companions had collapsed without a word onto the straw mattresses in the cottage. Now, in the early light, Mukta considered the rustic Scottish landscape. "I have heard of middle of nowhere, but never before have I seen it."

Natalie and Angelica still slept; Bucky and Sangita shuffled to the edge of the water, delighting in its utter clarity, apparent even before the sun had fully risen. Two sand smelt glided in the shallows, their movements made in tandem. An instant of perfect silence hung upon the water, then the sun broke over the hills behind them, filling the air with a delicate light, soon pierced by the cries of seabirds.

Bucky gestured toward the nearest ridge. "Let's climb up and see what's on the other side." They kicked through the damp grass and scrambled over the low outcroppings of lichen-covered stone, tramping up the rise to a crest where the view was revealed. Down the length of the island patches of sea spilled across the fields, sparkling under the pure rays of morning. In the distance, craggy towers like ancient fingers thrust up from the earth. It was not so much a country as a painter's vision of heaven, and overwhelmed by beauty and a sense of relief, he took Sangita's hand and held it tightly.

She turned to him. "We will have days here. We can explore this place together." An instant later she was in his arms.

At midweek a boat delivered food and drinks to their dock, along with a Glasgow newspaper. The greatest scandal since the Profumo affair had rocked the worlds of power and money, but after days of howling headlines, the story had migrated below the fold. An update dwelled on the infamous video, first shown at Cliveden. Soon located on a UK website, the clip had been uploaded to innumerable sites and blogs, tallying tens of millions of views in an endless chain of downloads. The newspaper noted the aftermath:

"Nicolai V. Klepakov, the man identified in the closing titles, appears to have left Britain. A flight plan filed at Farnborough Airport for a private jet chartered by the Dzerzhinsky Group, of which he is the majority shareholder, lists Doha, Qatar, as the intended destination. Attempts to reach Mr. Klepakov or a spokesman for comment have thus far failed. The woman seen in the video, believed to be Natalie Wells-Harvey, a British citizen, has not been located. Her website, www.KnottyNatalie.net, has been only intermittently available due to massive demand."

Bucky gathered the tired travelers. "We can go back to London on Friday, if you like."

Natalie and Angelica were keen to leave. But since arriving, Mukta had changed her mind about the Hebrides. "It is so lovely and peaceful here, I would be pleased to stay through the weekend."

Bucky nodded his agreement, then spoke with Natalie. "I still owe you some tactics, and here's the first. Whenever you can reach your Internet service provider, tell them you need the fattest pipe they've got in front of your website."

Since leaving London, Angelica had reverted to one of her

darker moods, her protective instincts triggered by the risks posed to Natalie. But with confirmation in hand that the oligarch had been driven out of Britain, she came to Bucky with her version of praise.

"I never thought you had the bollocks to bring off a stunt like this."

"What can I tell you? Klepakov fucked with the wrong geek." As she laughed and turned away, Bucky considered the four women, gathered together on the Scottish shore from the reaches of the old empire. Softly, but emphatically, his inner ear whispered, *My Newmanry.*

SEVENTEEN

Before evacuating from London, he had removed his computers, clothing and personal property from the Belgrave Square house, and handed over his keys to Yuri. He had no reason to return. But something—whether curiosity, or the sense that he owed his former partner a full explanation—led Bucky to return after several weeks. The house appeared unchanged as Laira opened the door; the great Entry Hall with its columns and mythic colonnade still stunned and uplifted all who entered, establishing a lofty tone for the sensual delights to follow. From the Grand Saloon above came the noise and bustle of the table games and the laughter of revelers at the crystal bar. Laira was chattering pleasantly, something about how hectic the life of the club had been, and as the energy of the house washed over him, Bucky recalled a warning from his first month in Manhattan: *If you want to see the hole you'll leave by quitting any company, shove your fist into a bucket of water and pull it out again.*

He asked about the girls. Were they thriving and content? Had anyone left the house? Laira told him the bittersweet news that Krassy and Sassy had returned to Sofia, to join a newly-formed Bulgarian troupe. They had left behind dozens of members who had grown to love their powerful takedowns and half nelsons, and their unforgettable spread-eagled aromatherapy. Charlotte, another original, had snared a gazillionaire with a taste for risky marriage. And Mandy had given notice that she would avoid the London winter by spending it back on Bondi Beach. Bucky waited, anticipating there might be more, but Laira understood the reason he had come. "He's in the Library." She pointed the way as if Bucky might have forgotten.

"Ah, *tovarish*," Yuri said cautiously, as he entered the room, "you have located serviceable flat?"

They sat down on opposite sides of the Italian reading table, at first with a shared sense of discomfort, then with growing warmth as they realized there was nothing to dispute or regret. Bucky ran his hand over the lustrous surface, remembering Sangita's first and only visit to the interior of the house. Out of necessity, he had said nothing about their meetings and clandestine acts, but now the whole story could be told—the truth about Klepakov's threats and bribes; the cyber war he had waged to upend brothel keepers and foment anonymous trouble; the brawling raid on the slave house at Luton; and, finally, how a wireless camera and a pimply boy had torpedoed the oligarch's plans. Yuri appeared desperate for a drink, but he listened silently. Almost as an afterthought, recalling his question about a flat, Bucky told him about the house he had rented in Ilford. The small but comfortable dwelling stood on a street that Sangita liked, close to a park with a lake, and not too far from her mother.

Yuri pushed back from the table as his eyes filled with understanding. "Perhaps astrologers are correct, and celestial bodies determine our fates. When love comes twice in one week, there can be no explanation but the stars."

"*Twice?*"

"You know that Natalie and Angelica share a unique affection...the kind that flows only between lovers who have found their ideal mates. Angelica is domme, Natalie is sub, should anyone be shocked by such a blissful couple? But now there is more. Angelica has no website, while Natalie has audience of millions. Together they hope to become most famous Internet film stars."

"They're made for each other. Most couples marry with less in common." As Bucky imagined the scorching videos that Angelica and Natalie would whip up together, he realized that he had never tallied the results of the promising start-ups launched from within their circle. International Fulfillment had flourished, and Klub Kloze had quickly failed, but Knotty-Natalie.net might well achieve the greatest success.

"Since we speak of trusted partners," said Yuri, "there are matters to resolve between us. Perhaps I placed too much faith in Nicolai Vasilievitch. It is a common mistake, when a powerful, older man helps one who is still in his youth. But you, *tovarish*, have never lied or let me down." He got to his feet and moved purposefully across the Library, motioning to Bucky to follow. On a circular table in the opposite corner, a yard of silk, darkly shining, had been draped over a hidden mass. The legs of the table were bowed beneath the weight. "Since the Boss's departure all house revenues have flowed to me. As Brits would say, it is no trifling sum. Is only fair that you receive just recompense for your work as founding partner, and your role in freeing us from the oligarch's heavy hand." He deftly pinched the silk cloth where it rose to a peak, sweeping it up and away in a magician's stage gesture.

On the table, hundreds of palladion coins had been stacked into a perfect pyramid. Yuri allowed a hint of conspiracy to enter his voice: "Since you will wonder, this is half of the second horde, minted as gifts for supporters. As currency they have no value. But melted down to bullion, each ounce has considerable worth."

Bucky muttered a lame attempt at thanks, stunned by the sudden riches. He had thrown a day pack over his shoulder before setting out from Ilford. He emptied it of a sweater, a sandwich, and a water bottle, and began to sweep the coins from the table into the sack.

"Taxi may be best for your return," Yuri advised, as if he were recommending the proper shingles for a roofing job. "Combined weight of coins is thirty-seven point eight kilos, hardly an impossible burden for a strong young man, but I think it unwise to go about on the Tube with such treasure. Many men are less honest than you and me."

▪ ▪ ▪

With December, a winter chill descended over London, but the New Year Honours List brought a wonderful surprise. Sangita would receive an MBE for her charity work. She was speechless with astonishment, but Mukta Sharma burst into joyous tears at the news.

"Who could imagine, my daughter a Member of the British Empire? What a husband you will be able to find now!"

Sangita waited a day before explaining that her choice had already been made.

Knowing nothing about the nature of the award, Bucky was less than thrilled; the Honours List named civil servants and dairy farmers from Redding to Rotorua, merchants and military officers, opera singers and railroad executives, even long-suffering college dons. Whatever respect the honorees had earned, it was no Roman conquerors' parade, and he thought that a civil distinction mattered little when compared to the practical impact of Devi Way's work. But during the weeks before the investiture something more exciting diverted his attention. Jackie Wax became a tabloid hero.

On a night off, Wax visited a pub in the West End where the burly Corporal Hobart had found weekend work as a bouncer. All was calm, a bit noisy but without a hint of trouble, and they stood at the bar, drinking and reminiscing about their days in the Paras, paying only slight attention to the midevening crowd. Wax showed off his cast with pride. The bones in his hand had been slow to heal, and the bulky white mass still clung to his wrist, weeks after he had expected to be rid of it. His doctor had suggested that substituting milk for the beer in his diet might speed the healing process, but Wax saw no merit in this. Instead he grudgingly agreed to wear the stained contraption for a final two weeks.

Around eleven, after the theaters had run down their curtains, a distinguished middle-aged man entered, accompanied by a younger woman—one of the minor royals and his daughter. Oddly, they had come in without a protective detail. Wax and Hobart watched as a circle formed around them—everyone clamoring to buy them drinks—and from snatches of the conversation they realized that the Princess had reached legal age only that week. The night out was a small celebration.

More of the after-theater crowd poured in. An outsize man in a magnificent suit pushed his way forward to the bar, to the right of the royals. He had a head of disheveled white hair and a beak-like nose that gave him the look of a fish eagle. Beneath the nose was something less like a mouth than a maw. "Gin," he called to the bartender, pointing to the Plymouth bottle, "and just a drop of tonic." When the glass came he tossed back a slug with a satisfied "Haaah!" then turned to his left. "Enjoying the evening, Your Royal Highnesses?"

"Indeed we are, thank you," said the Prince.

"Tonight was my first time for *Les Mis*," the Princess added. "It was bloody marvelous. Have you seen it?"

"Bit of a Bolshevik slant for my taste, all that ridiculous business on the barricades. Just the sort of nonsense you'd expect of the Frogs."

"Ah yes, I take your point," the Prince replied, canny enough not to argue.

But the Princess still felt a revolutionary wind at her back, or at least the liberating effects of her first West End glass. "I understood it as a tale about the love between generations. I don't think that has anything to do with Bolshevism. Did you see another show?"

"Not a show, precisely, I attended a performance of *Mrs. Warren's Profession.*"

"I see, well, each to their own."

Another swig of gin disappeared, then the white-haired man went on. "I prefer theater that presents the masses in an honest light. Despite what certain starry-eyed librettists might have you believe, the great unwashed is no collection of Christian martyrs."

"See here," the Prince protested, "there's no need to be uncharitable."

"Nor dishonest, Your Royal Highness. Particularly when Darwin assures us that the cream shall surely rise, whether among *Homo sapiens* or the lesser animal species."

Now the Princess didn't bother to hide her annoyance. "Whatever are you talking about?"

"I am speaking of the mechanisms that control our lives, whether in love or commerce."

"What makes you think the laws of love and the laws of commerce have anything in common?"

The big man laughed as if a child had uttered some naïve notion. "Let me offer you an example of a law that works as well for both. It makes no difference whether you're the buyer or seller; it makes *all* the difference whether you're the fucker or fuckee."

Hobart had drawn closer, lurking as the exchange veered from bad to worse. Now he seized the blowhard's arm. "That's enough out of you. Come along!" Given the man's age, the last thing Hobart expected was physical resistance, but the drinking hand came up in a flash, and half a glass of straight gin shot into his eyes. He cursed at the blinding sting, turned and clawed for a handhold but lost his grip, then tripped and went down, banging his forehead against a table.

Morley Cruikshank never saw the circular loop traced by Wax's heavy cast. The plaster mitt rose up behind him and curved to clear the ceiling, then descended on his cranium like a boulder dropped from a castle keep. As he fell, Wax seized the back of his belt. With the enormous strength of his right arm, he hoisted Cruikshank horizontally, then bulled his way to the door and launched him into Rupert Street. A gaggle of paparazzi waited, tipped that the Prince and his daughter had entered. In the morning the shot of the day graced the front of every London paper: a coldcocked man with a raptor's face, heaved headlong into the gutter as the royals looked on in awe. One of the rags added a caption below the photo: "'Ere, guv'nor, let me help you to your coach!"

■ ■ ■

Bucky had arranged for Will Beard to drive Sangita and her mother to the Palace on the afternoon of the investiture. Sangita insisted that the Duchess be invited as well, and that Bucky accompany their party. He expected the familiar black cab, but Beard pulled up in a majestic silvery Daimler, borrowed from the carriage house at Westerley Park. Had it been a living being, the vehicle might have been the grandfather to Yuri's lost Bentley—slower, less agile, and lacking any computerized toys, but a marvel of craftsmanship and motoring refinement. The Duchess sat beside Beard in the passenger seat, resplendent in a woolen ensemble and an art deco diamond brooch; she played absent-mindedly with the plain gold engagement ring that Will had given her.

"We thought this might be more suitable transport, in view of the state occasion," Beard explained.

Sangita introduced her mother to the Duchess, noting, "Her Grace has been extremely generous in her support of Devi Way."

"You must be terribly proud of your daughter, Mrs. Sharma. My congratulations to you both, on Sangita receiving honors."

"Thank you, Your Grace. It's actually Miss Sharma, Sangita's father and I never married."

Beard jumped in to save them. "These are modern times, and we must all adapt. Isn't that right, darling?"

"Indeed we must, Wills. Mr. Newman, I understand that you have taken up residence in Ilford. It must be quite an adjustment after your time at Belgrave Square."

"Hey, I'm liking it, Your Grace. Ilford isn't that different from the neighborhood where I grew up. And I needed to be in the area to supervise the renovation of our women's shelter—there's a lot to do. The weird part is, after I left Belgravia, things started becoming much clearer to me. I think I'm finally beginning to understand this country."

Beard objected. "That may be premature; what you now believe to be the essence of things is more likely superficial. England is not the hills and fields, nor the laws or our religion. It is not the estates and gardens, the factories and ports, our history, our literature, or even our people."

"What then?"

The wise cabbie paused for time, his brow deeply furrowing until he was certain he had found the right words. "'England is a passing glimmer in the mind, when material and metaphysical coalesce in wonder.'"

The Duchess threw up her hands. "That's spat on, Wills! I couldn't have put it better."

In the Palace ballroom, rows of chairs had been carefully arranged on a rich burgundy carpet for subjects chosen to receive honors. Families sat in double ranks of benches like choir pews that extended down the long walls. The Lord Chamberlain, two Gurkha officers and five Yeomen of the Guard accompanied the sovereign; after the anthem, the Lord Chamberlain began to intone each name, and the achievements of that woman or man: "services to aircraft design…services to secondary education… services to the retail trade." When Sangita's name was called, with the credit, "for services to charity," her mother's eyes over-flowed. Bucky took her hand until Sangita, returning from the dais, paused before them to hold up the award for their view. Below the red ribbon was a polished metal cross, and an inner circle stamped with the profiles of George V and his queen.

More than one hundred received their due, and the ceremony appeared about to end. But there had been a late addition to the Honours List. The lord chamberlain, staring impassively, droned, "Algernon J. Wax, for services to the beverage trade." An oaken cask of a man in an ill-fitting suit lumbered forward, his spiky hair slicked up in points, an expression of unaccustomed bewilderment straining his face. He bent forward, whispering, "Very grateful, mum," as a small woman with sharp eyes pinned a decoration to his massive chest.

Months later, on a balmy Sunday soon after their wedding, Bucky and Sangita came in from Ilford to enjoy the first warm weekend of spring. The city bloomed with dewy flower beds and verdant lawns and gardens; after the long winter Londoners had come out in millions, filling the parks and squares, parading in shirt sleeves along the avenues from Knightsbridge to Mayfair. Maybe it was the rising barometric pressure, but whatever the cause, Bucky hadn't felt so high in weeks, even in the afterglow of the honeymoon. Not a single thing in his life was amiss.

They were strolling up Brompton Road toward Harrods, navigating the throngs on the sidewalks, when Yuri Pavlovitch Dolgorukov motored past in a respectable Fiat. A handsome round-faced woman in sunglasses stared from the passenger seat, and three brawny boys jostled in the back. Bucky waved and called out to them, but perhaps dreading the explanation he would owe his wife, Yuri pretended not to notice. Bucky sensed that it might be the last time he would see his former partner, and he reached for his phone, certain he still had Yuri's number saved.

"Who?" Sangita asked.

"Someone I met in my second week in London."

"A friend?"

He hesitated, palming the phone as he waited to see if Yuri would circle back, but the Fiat rolled on out of sight. He put the phone away. "In the end he was."

Sangita smiled, content with this answer, needing nothing more.

For a moment Bucky experienced a sweet, sad feeling that he had never known before—a pang of nostalgia for the younger man he had been, in those early days in London. The recollection washed over him in a tidal ebb and flow of emotions, like the mixing of fresh and salt waters in the estuary of the Thames. Then, recalling why they had walked from the V&A, it all resolved and made magical sense, beyond any boyish need for logical explanations. He took Sangita's arm and allowed her to guide him through the polished doors of the great store and on to the eternal joys of the food courts.